Murray Smith, who wrote scripts for BULMAN, and STRANGERS before it, is a long-established television and film writer. He lives in Sussex.

Robert Holdstock is the author of the science fiction novels EARTHWIND, WHERE TIME WINDS BLOW, NECROMANCER and MYTHAGO WOOD. He lives in Hertfordshire.

Also available from Futura

BULMAN

ROBERT HOLDSTOCK

Bulman 2

One of our Pigeons is missing

A novel from scripts
written by MURRAY SMITH

George Bulman is based on the original character created by KENNETH ROYCE in THE XYY MAN and other novels published by Hodder & Stoughton

Futura

A Futura Book

First published in Great Britain in 1984 by
Futura Publications,
a Division of Macdonald & Co (Publishers) Ltd
London & Sydney

ISBN 0 7088 2716 0

Typeset, printed and bound in Great Britain by
Hazell Watson and Viney Limited,
Member of the BPCC Group,
Aylesbury, Bucks

Futura Publications
A Division of
Macdonald & Co (Publishers) Ltd
Maxwell House
74 Worship Street
London EC2A 2EN
A BPCC plc Company

PART ONE

The Name of the Game

Chapter One

Standing in the shadows . . .

To a cat, prowling the grey streets of Limehouse on this bleak, drizzling dawn, the man standing huddled in the dark security of a doorway was as clear as if he had been standing in full daylight. A dog would have noticed him instantly by his smell, the odour of tiredness, and sweat, and impatience. A remote radar surveillance monitor could also have picked him out, as patterns of heat and cold, digitalized squares of colour, moving and shifting as the man shuffled his position, cramped and cold from the long night's watching.

To ordinary human eyes, of course, he was quite invisible, a dark shape within darkness, not even the glow of a cigarette end or the flash of light on open eyes being allowed to betray his presence.

He was far too much an expert in the art of concealment for that to happen.

He was a stocky man, in his late forties, whose face was hard when he was angry, but could become almost impish when he was amused. His dark hair was cropped short, although he wore his sideburns unfashionably long. He was huddled inside a thick leather jacket, its collar turned up against the cold and the miserable, relentless drizzle. As he suffered, so he consoled himself by murmuring fatalistic lines from the works of William Shakespeare.

The quality of sleuthing is not strained, it droppeth as a ton of bricks upon the unsuspecting villain . . .

Come on Greenstein, you ponce; show your face. I've got a clock to mend!

George Bulman had spent more hours on this sort of waiting and watching assignment than he cared to remember. Twenty years a copper, and probably as much as five of those had been spent huddled in alleys, or behind dustbins, or on rooftops, a flask of coffee by one hand, a regulation issue pistol by the other, the cold and damp seeping through his clothes.

But in those days, when he had been with the Metropolitan Police, there had been a sense of comradeship, of support. It had been more like an elaborate game. Four hours in the cold, and then some fresh-faced constable would crawl up to him and whisper, 'Take an hour, guv, and get a cup of tea. I'll stand in.' Or, when he was with the InterCity Group and standing around in strange towns (just as cold, just as damp) he could usually count on the cheerful features of young Derek Willis, grinning at him from some other vantage point.

Get your head down, Willis, you monkey . . . they can see you from Denmark!

He thought again how much he missed Willis. He missed them all, really; Lambie, Willis . . . all of them. Life, for George Bulman, was very different now. He was alone, and without a back-up group. A Private Investigator's lot was a very solitary one. No brown bags of sandwiches, no flasks of tea, no eager young coppers glancing to him for reassurance.

Alone on the streets. Cold on the streets. Wet on the streets.

Waiting for a monkey called Elias Greenstein to step nimbly out of the front door of the Maritime Shipping Company's office, across the road.

The shipping office was a small, unremarkable building, mostly red brick and windows, standing in a wide, deserted yard just off the gloomy Rhodeswell Road with its tall, Victorian dwellings and deserted warehouses.

Bulman had seen movement behind one of the shipping office's windows during the night, and was confident that his hunch about the elusive American, Greenstein, was correct. It made him feel proud. His pursuit of the man had been one of the longest and most difficult assignments he had yet undertaken in his new life as a P.I.

But the moment was at hand. Greenstein would leave the building, and it would be the short, brisk walk, the hand on the shoulder, the smile of triumph and the citizen's arrest . . .

Only one thing rankled. Only one thing clouded the perfection of the operation.

It was in the shape of a battered 5 cwt van, parked farther down the road, an unremarkable vehicle, one of thousands of the same. Its presence, nevertheless, was irking Bulman deeply. He had been too long a copper not to recognize a surveillance vehicle. Though the van looked deserted, twice during the early morning he had seen it move slightly, as the men inside shifted about in cramped discomfort.

Probably police, or perhaps Customs, or some Ministry's heavies . . . who could tell? The likeliest bet was the Flying Squad. But if it was Fraud, then maybe they too were after Elias Greenstein, and that rankled. Bulman had worked too hard and too long to have his thunder stolen now. This was *his* case. The long arm of the law had damn well better snap into a polite salute.

Come on! Let's get it over with.

Then he stiffened up again, and listened hard.

Distantly there was the sound of a car's engine, revving low, approaching the scene of the stake-out in a slow, deliberate way.

Moving carefully through the cramped space at the back of the van, Dennis Holmes crouched for the tenth time by the small observation slit in the rear doors.

Peering hard into the grey, rainy dawn he searched the view so afforded with a suspicious and cautious eye. Behind him, Jim Benson and Dave Rogers huddled inside their zip-up jackets, cold and hungry, fed-up with life and with this operation. Benson kept checking his hand-gun, and the nervous, neurotic action was making Dave Rogers increasingly edgy.

'I'm telling you . . .' Holmes said for the fourth time in twenty minutes. 'There's a geezer standing in that doorway. I know it. I can feel it.'

He watched the dark entrance. Even in full daylight the deeper recess of the doorway, leading into a deserted office block, would have been obscured in shadow. He could see no movement. He had nothing visual to go on.

'Hallucinations,' Benson said. 'You need to get your blood sugar up. Start imagining things and we'll start shooting at cloud shadows.'

'That bloody cat,' Holmes said. 'It keeps looking at the doorway. There's someone there.'

The cat, a grey tabby, saturated with rain but apparently unconcerned, was playing and preening in full view. Every so often it rolled onto its back and played kick and chase games with the air. Then it would sit up and stare at the doorway.

D.I. Holmes knew he was right. There was a man in the shadows, watching them.

'Rain. Bloody rain. Why does it always bloody rain?' The words of frustration, expressed by Jim Benson, accompanied an increase in the drum-beat patter of rain on the van's roof.

'Doesn't look like chummy's showing up anyhow,' Rogers murmured. He scratched his face and zipped his windcheater up tighter. He was the youngest of the three, and looked the most tired.

Holmes changed position, peering towards the Maritime Shipping Company's office, and at the sleek, red Bentley that was parked at its side. The car shimmered with the light and the rain that was falling on it. Holmes idly wondered what its owner – one Elias Greenstein – was doing, working through the night without a light visible in any of the offices. Holmes had a suspicious mind, and any abnormal behaviour made him think long and hard, but usually without coming to any firm conclusion.

But Greenstein was not their worry at the moment. If Holmes had any worry at all it was that Tait was not going to show.

He could hardly bear the thought. All night on a tip-off, all night in the cold and the rain, waiting for a blagging that they were *sure* was going down . . .

But it was the name of the game. Tip-offs could work both ways. If Tait had got wind that his latest plan had been leaked to the police, then right now he would be lazing in bed, a smug, self-satisfied grin on his face, imagining the environmental agonies of his least favourite copper.

Distantly there was the sound of a car's engine. Holmes allowed the merest flicker of a smile to play upon his lips. He patted his breast, where the bulky shape of his Smith and Wesson was a comforting weight. Benson grabbed the radio microphone from the small panel at the side of the van, and switched it on.

Static crackled. The three men shifted to the thin observation slits, and held their breath.

'It's them,' Benson whispered as a cream XJ-6 Jaguar slid slowly into view. The windows were darkened. The car slowed as it approached, then slid more rapidly along the road and turned into the yard of the Maritime Shipping Company.

'Oh . . . dead cocky. Going straight in . . .' Holmes drew out his pistol as he spoke. He glanced at Benson. 'Detail Bob Mitchell's motor to block off that yard entrance.'

'Rats in a trap . . .' Rogers whispered. He was shaking slightly.

'Not yet they ain't.'

The Jaguar pulled around inside the yard, so that it stood facing the open gate. It kept its motor running. Three doors opened and three men stepped out into the grey dawn. Holmes had time enough to glimpse the familiar features of Dodger Tait, one of old Bernie Scroop's closest allies on the street, before all three villains had tugged on black balaclava masks. They ran quickly to the main entrance to the Shipping Offices, and Holmes saw light reflect off the shortened barrel of a shotgun.

'Bird gun,' he said quietly.

Benson said, 'Yeah. I saw it.' He looked at Holmes. 'You scared, guv?'

Holmes smiled thinly and shook his head. 'Nah. I love it. Food and drink . . .' And he turned and wiped a finger along his upper lip; the finger came away wet. He grinned. 'Not scared a bit.'

What in the Lordly name of the Good Will Shakespeare was *going on?*

George Bulman watched the Jaguar sidle towards him, and then turn into the Maritime building's yard, and allowed himself the luxury of a single, audible curse. The car – cream, M registration, showing signs of having been resprayed – was familiar to him, though not so familiar that he could put a name or a face to the owner.

But if a car shouted its identity like this one had, then one thing was for sure: the man behind the reflecting windscreen was no Jesuit Priest.

As the three men jumped swiftly from the Jaguar, now turned about inside the yard itself, Bulman felt irritation rise to fury levels. Damn and double damn, he thought, or words to that effect. A blagging going on right under his nose, and a van-load of edgy coppers waiting to pounce like mangy cats upon their three unsuspecting rats, and all he, George Bulman, wanted was to earn an honest day's living by fulfilling the task for which he had been paid, and for which he had waited out the night, namely the citizen's arrest of an insurance trickster.

What the hell to do now? Back off and let the more serious arrest take place, and risk losing Greenstein?

No way.

'Be bloody, bold and resolute,' he intoned softly. 'Laugh to scorn the power of Sweeney . . .'

Yes indeed. Be resolute. It was the name of the game, in any case.

Good old Will.

The three men had disappeared inside the building. The Jaguar kept its motor running. Bulman watched edgily and nervously, risking exposure – in the visual sense – by trying to peer far enough into the day to scan the small side-entrance to the offices.

It was as well he did.

'*Gotcha* my son!'

Elias Greenstein had slipped from the building like a wraith. He was a small man, in his fifties, with silvery hair, and silver-framed glasses. He was wearing a light-coloured, camel-hair coat and carried a thin black briefcase. He glanced quickly around as he locked the side door, then walked with indecent haste towards his Bentley. In the drizzling rain he managed to almost merge with every background feature. He radiated guilt and conspiracy with every well-heeled step.

Bulman shrugged up his coat collar, glanced at the green Bedford van, and stepped from hiding.

Blood, bold and resolute . . .

He walked swiftly towards Greenstein, entering the Shipping Office's gates and not even glancing at the purring XJ-6, trying not to think too hard about how startled, how alarmed, the invisible man in the driver's seat must have been.

Be bloody, be bold . . .

'Elias Greenstein?' he called loudly, and the small man in the expensive coat stopped in alarm, and stared at the approaching stranger. He clutched his briefcase harder, Bulman noticed. His right hand, holding his car keys, was white with tension.

Then, from inside the building, came the sound of a shot. A gunshot. It stopped Bulman dead in his tracks, and Greenstein too showed signs of alarm. Both men stared at the red brick building, then slowly back at each other.

Bulman stepped forward . . . *Bloody, bold and res–*

Two more shots sounded. A window exploded outwards, a shower of bright glass in the bright rain.

Bloody hell!

Greenstein quickly turned to his car and fumbled at the lock. Bulman ran over to him, head reeling, mind racing. There was heavy duty going down inside the building, and common sense told him to get the hell out of the combat zone. But he'd hunted Greenstein too long. The prey was in his sights. He couldn't backtrack now . . .

He caught up with Greenstein and reached to the man's shoulder, jerking him back just as he was about to get into the driver's seat of his Bentley. 'A little word, Mister Greenstein.'

Greenstein, caught, resorted to indignation. 'Who the hell are you?' He stared furiously at George Bulman, but the fire of anger in his grey eyes couldn't mask the waters of panic. The American was petrified.

'I'm acting on behalf of the Union Atlantic Banking Corporation. They are, as you can imagine, intrigued to learn how you managed to swindle them out of two and a half million dollars.'

The look in Greenstein's eyes told Bulman that the little man could imagine all too well how intrigued the big City banks were by his activities.

Another shot, then the slamming of doors. The sound of men running, the sound of a man shouting. The Jaguar revved its engine, a sound that spoke of fear and panic felt by the man who sat behind the wheel.

'I don't know what you're talking about,' Greenstein stammered, but his attention was only half on Bulman. He appeared transfixed by the sights and sounds of the raid.

'You're a trickly ponce, Greenstein,' Bulman said, in mock admiration. 'But you can't hide from–'

His words of triumph were rudely interrupted by the screech of tyres on wet ground, and the sudden, deafening roar of an engine pushed to breaking point. The Jaguar almost skidded as it accelerated from its stationary mode, then veered to avoid a large Bedford van that had suddenly appeared from nowhere to block the gates.

The Jaguar span on the soaking ground and rammed the van sideways on. Its doors flew open and four men scrambled for the dawn. The rear doors of the Bedford were half opened, then kicked fully out, one of them hanging limp by a single hinge.

Greenstein and Bulman watched open-mouthed as five plain-clothes policemen tumbled out, wielding pick-handles and pistols.

There was much shouting. Men scattered. Men chased. The cat watched from across the road.

As he turned back to Greenstein, from the corner of his eye he noticed three men walking towards the Shipping Yard from the green Bedford that had been parked all night. He thought he recognized one of the coppers, but the stray thought was broken by the look of fierce survival that had suddenly crept into the eyes of his own victim.

'The game's up, Elias. Time to accept that you will no longer be passing GO . . .'

'You *bastard!*' Greenstein shouted, and the sudden violence in his voice startled Bulman, despite the running battle behind him. He never saw Greenstein's briefcase until it struck him on the side of the head. A slim little bag, of soft leather, whatever Greenstein was carrying had the weight and feel of a brick. It made Bulman dizzy for a second, and he staggered against the side of the Bentley. When he straightened up, Greenstein was in full flight, through the tussle of police and crooks. Bulman pursued him.

It was like running through the Battle of Agincourt. His most vivid image, as he weaved and dodged in the wake of the surprisingly nimble smaller man, was of sticks rising and falling with sickening, crunching thuds, and of men dodging and ducking, as if engaged in the most honourable of jousting tournaments.

Then the ground hit him in the face, with a sickening and jarring shock, and the sudden bitter taste of blood in his mouth. Too stunned for a second to realize what had happened, Bulman struggled helplessly against what felt like the binding of ropes around his ankles.

He pushed himself up onto his elbows, and was rudely pushed down again, the hand on the back of his head applied with excessive force so that his other cheek was bruised on the wet tarmac.

'Stay down chummy or you'll walk with a stick for the rest of your life . . .'

'Let me up. He's getting away!'

Bulman's feeble protests did no more than earn him a savage punch to the right kidney, which sent pain through his whole torso. His hands were behind his back, and cold metal snapped around the wrists. The same man dragged him to his feet by his forearms so that his shoulders were nearly dislocated. Around him the four men from the Jaguar were being led, still struggling, to the van that had blocked the gate. Bulman was pushed after them.

'I'm nothing to do with this!' he shouted, struggling in the fierce grip of the young detective. He didn't recognize the lad's face, but features were not clear on anyone at the moment, being liberally painted with rain and blood.

'Shaddup!' the copper said, and pushed him harder. Bulman smarted all over from the flying tackle that had brought him down. The policeman looked small, but every time he squeezed Bulman's flesh it sent arrows of pain through the older man's muscles.

All part of the training, he remembered grimly. Know how to hurt, and apply pain, and keep the pain coming without tiring your own muscles.

He was jostled to the van. He protested once more.

'I'm an ex-copper. Come on, laddie, who's in charge of this oppo? Get 'em over here.'

There was no response. He was jammed against the door of the van, which one of the Met's younger policemen had now fixed.

'Get inside. *Laddie!*' Bulman was helped on his way with a touch of stick around his thighs.

Oh you *vicious* bastard, he thought grimly, and stared hard at the copper, at the fresh face, the narrowed eyes, the grazed cheeks, the grin . . . always the grin on this sort of young monkey, as if being in the Force somehow gave them the right to make their own rules of combat.

Then he saw Greenstein.

A detective – his back to Bulman – was just giving Elias Greenstein back his briefcase. Greenstein was smiling and nodding. He indicated the building, then shrugged. He made an expression of bewilderment. The detective wrote something down. Bulman could imagine everything . . .

It happened behind me. I knew nothing about it. Of course I'll be available for a statement, but I don't think I can help. I was working through the night, with some colleagues. All a great shock. Wish I could help more. In the briefcase? Just some papers, rather confidential . . .

Oh yes, Greenstein. You are a *tricky* ponce . . .

The young copper was about to bang the door of the van closed, locking Bulman and the four villains away in the dark. Greenstein was walking to his Bentley, walking jauntily, Bulman thought, tossing his keys up and down in his right hand.

'I'm telling you,' Bulman said loudly. 'I'm nothing to do with this caper. I don't know who you are, sonny, or what outfit you're with, but I'm ex-Detective Chief Inspector George Bulman!'

The copper smiled and nodded. 'Turn round and I'll take the cuffs off. But no monkey business.'

Bulman did as he'd been told, but gasped with frustration. 'I'm telling you!' he began, and had been about to say to the hard-faced crook sitting next to him, '*You* tell 'em!' when he realized just *who* it was he was sitting next to.

'Dodger Tait . . .' he murmured. The cuffs came free and he massaged his wrists gratefully. Tait stared at him, a supercilious grin on his face. He was bleeding from a small cut below his short, fair hair, but his face, an angular, evil mask, was just as Bulman remembered it. The eyes that could watch violence as easily as they watched a cricket match, and with the same indifference.

'Mister Bulman,' Tait breathed quietly, delightedly. 'Well I never.'

Recovering from his surprise at coming face to face with such an old adversary under such adverse conditions, Bulman made a last effort to make the arresting officer see sense.

As the door was closed on the back of the van, two other coppers crawling in to sit among the villains, Bulman said, 'I used to work for the InterCity Unit. Jack Lambie's lot. I'm a P.I., now, employed by Union Atlantic. I'm not *with* this bunch!'

Tait laughed in the background. The young policeman, still clearly pleased with his part in the arrest, hesitated for a moment before locking the van door. He glanced at Tait and said, 'What about it, Tait? Is he one of you or what?'

Dodger Tait chuckled even louder. 'Old Georgie? 'Course he is. Just 'aving a touch of bottle trouble, that's all. Chin up, Georgie.'

The door slammed closed.

No sooner had the police transit van lurched off towards the nearest station, than Bulman was handcuffed again, this time to Tait. He sat and listened to the siren wailing, vaguely aware of the flashing blue lights that announced the convoy's passage.

The ignominy of his arrest had been made worse by Tait's gleeful sneering, but now the crook sat in brooding silence, staring at the two police who rode in the back with them.

The van swayed and rocked, giving Bulman the usual uncomfortable ride on the hard seats. But usually it had been *him* with the keys to the handcuffs, sitting watching the crestfallen features of men who now knew they faced eight or ten years in cold, stark cells.

After a few minutes Bulman regained his composure, and felt a lessening of his irritation. Greenstein was gone. For the moment. He'd find him again. What worried him now was just how many hours it was going to take before a familiar face walked by and realized that a mistake had been made by the over-enthusiastic arresting officer.

He turned to the dark features of Dodger Tait. 'What was the point of dropping me in it, Dodger? Eh? You'll only make things worse for yourself.'

Tait looked at him, a thin, humourless smile on his lips. 'Firstly, Georgie, you're a bastard. I enjoyed it. Right?'

'Fair enough.'

'Second.' Tait shrugged. 'Worse? That's a joke, right Georgie? I've been nicked on a blagging with a bird gun clutched in my warm little hands. And ten square feet of shot-peppered plaster to show what a good aim I've got. Come on, George. I'm off down the steps for a cock an' hen.'

Bulman shrugged and looked away. 'Yeah, well you ain't done yourself no favours, Dodger.'

'True enough,' said Dodger Tait, as the van swayed and he was thrown closer to Bulman. 'So we'd better try something else . . .'

The words themselves were enough of an alarm to make Bulman tense, ready for trouble. He should have sensed it coming! For some seconds Tait had been fiddling with his ankle, apparently scratching an itch.

If Bulman hadn't been so damned distracted by losing Greenstein, and being cuffed to an ex-con under suspicion himself, he might have pre-empted the action that Tait now took. As it was, he could do nothing but stiffen, hold his breath, and pray that the van didn't go over a heavy bump in the road.

Dodger Tait had one of the most nervous trigger fingers that it had been George Bulman's dubious privilege to ease into submission.

And right now that itchy finger was curled around the trigger of a ·22 snub-nosed revolver.

The business end of the pistol, that cold and icy barrel end – *that metal O* – was rammed hard against his right ear, whispering sounds to him, the sound of the van's engine, the sound of Tait's breathing, the sound of blood, pulsing in thin-walled veins. For a while George Bulman listened to the sounds that might so easily turn out to be Death's overture, magnified by the hollow tube of the barrel.

As the two policemen in the back of the van tensed for action, Tait's voice rasped out, 'Easy, lads. Easy. We don't want a dead ex-Detective Chief Inspector on our hands. Or do we?'

There was a long silence, filled only by the rumble of the engine, the wail of the siren, and the sound of heavy breathing. Bulman watched the rear door of the van, feeling the steady pressure of the revolver on his temple, noticing how unwavering that pressure was.

After a moment he asked, 'How did the vote go?'

'Shut up,' Tait said, then snapped to one of the coppers, 'Keys. Come on, quickly. Quickly.' When the men hesitated the pressure on Bulman's head increased. Tait murmured evilly, 'Do tell 'em, Georgie. Do tell 'em that I mean it.'

Bulman smiled. 'He means it, lads. Dodger Tait'll squeeze the trigger as easy as squeezing a spot. He's married to Bennie Scroop's daughter. He's got friends in low places, you might say.'

A few seconds later there was the sound of handcuffs coming off. The gun remained by Bulman's ear. 'Okay,' Tait said. 'One of you bang on the cab panel. The signal to stop. No funny business. Brains on metalwork are sods to clean off.'

Three bangs on the partition between the rear and the cab, and the transit van slowed and pulled over to the side. The moment its wheels hit the kerb, even before it had stopped, Tait had kicked open the back doors, twisted round and jumped for the street. The moment the evil gun barrel was directed away from him, Bulman straightened and blocked the escape path for Tait's colleagues. He tussled with one while the others flung punches a. the police.

The green 5 cwt van that had staked out the Maritime Building skidded to avoid Tait's scampering figure. As Bulman struggled to hold his man, half in and half out of the transit, he saw two plain-clothes men leap from the green vehicle and pursue the running man.

One of them was D.I. Dennis Holmes, not one of Bulman's favourite coppers. He must have been in on the stake-out all the time, and Bulman just hadn't seen him.

There was a trickle of people on the east London streets, and a few cars sidling past the scene of the break-out.

Bulman watched helplessly as a minor tragedy was played to the end.

Tait must have known that he had nothing to lose by making the break, and risking twenty years instead of ten in the nick. He'd already spent a third of his life behind bars; if he went down now he'd be fifty before he saw daylight again, and Karen Scroop wouldn't wait that long.

Life had been shaping up nicely. If the blagging had worked, then with the haul from the Maritime he and Karen could have skipped off to Spain, bought one of the villas that – over the years – had been set up for people just like him, and lived happily in the sun, the only form of heat he relished.

But Fate had had it in for him. He'd not been unprepared. The pistol in his waistband had been his insurance, and he knew just how to stand when being searched so that quick, nervous hands would miss the armoury.

Nothing to lose. Everything to gain. Kill a copper or no, it was all the same now.

He ran along the street, conscious of the shouting of men behind him. He bowled two people aside roughly, but made tracks for pedestrians whenever he could. That, at least, would stop the police from shooting.

Then he saw the girl in the car . . . it was a new Escort, and she looked puzzled, frightened, a little stunned. She had stopped the car, nervous of driving past the flashing lights of the police vehicles.

Dodger Tait ran over to her in a second, jammed the revolver against her head and dragged her from the car. She didn't scream . . . she choked, a pale stream of vomit splashing down her pristine silk blouse.

Tait pushed her roughly aside as he jumped into the driver's seat and began to reverse down the road at nearly forty miles an hour. The pursuing figure of Dennis Holmes receded into the distance.

Then: more lights, more bloody blue lights!

The white transit careered round a corner, skidded to avoid Tait's reversing Escort, and the two vehicles collided and span out of control. The Escort struck a lamp-post. The engine died, and after two frantic attempts to start it up again, Tait abandoned the task as hopeless.

He stepped out onto the pavement, the revolver a hot presence in his right hand. He felt astonishingly cool and calm. His finger on the trigger was steady, though the rest of his body had started to tremble and sweat like a man with a fever.

'Leave it out, Tait!' Holmes called as he came closer. The copper was walking, now, a confident, slow step. He held his Smith and Wesson in two hands, but the barrel was pointed down at the kerb, an invitation to Tait to give up with honour.

'You stay back!' Tait shouted, looking around frantically.

There was a policeman behind him. The man had been creeping towards him along the edge of the shops and in the confusion Tait hadn't noticed.

He reacted without thinking, snapping off two shots from his ·22, and watching as the man ducked, then jerked, his face twisted into a grim mask of agony.

Then the policeman seemed to loom closer. The daylight grew darker, and there was an odd roaring in Tait's ears. Three dull thuds seemed to make the air contort and twist. The building ahead of him shuddered and spiralled, its perspectives changing, leaning close to him, then away.

Oddly, he seemed to be staring at the cold, hard pavement. He could see the cracked grain of the slab, the thin line of London dirt that had accumulated between adjacent flagstones.

What's happening? What's going on? Where am I?

His lungs wouldn't move. Warmth filled his mouth; it spilled, an expanding crimson lake, across the harsh white pavement.

Bees droned. Voices whispered.

Night fell.

Chapter Two

The moment Lucy McGinty stepped into Nicko's Greek cafe, and saw George Bulman sitting morosely in the far corner, she knew that things had gone very badly wrong. She steeled herself for a confrontation in which she would have to temper her cheerful optimism with sensitive reassurance.

Bulman looked as if his own private storm was raging about his head: dark, gloomy, bedraggled.

She ordered a coffee from the neatly turned-out man behind the bar, and made a face, asking, 'How long's he been here?'

Nicko shrugged, rolled his eyes.

It was bad, all right.

Coffee in her hand, Lucy walked carefully over to her boss, and sat down opposite him. When he glanced up she gave him a cheery smile. She was an attractive and vibrant young woman, in her early twenties, and looked every inch a Scot. Her father, the late Tom McGinty, had been a close friend of George Bulman's in the Met. It had been Tom McGinty's dream to end his days as a private investigator, and when Bulman had retired from the force, Lucy had almost single-handedly transferred her father's dream to her father's friend.

George Bulman had wanted to retire and work with clocks. Now he found himself mending clocks in the snatched moments between private investigation cases.

They made a good team, McGinty and Bulman. Lucy had her father's instinct for the streets, and for getting information from people. She worked hard and was almost impossible to disillusion, or depress.

Her very presence had an enlivening effect upon George Bulman.

He told her quickly what had happened, how he had blown the Greenstein caper, and how he had found himself arrested with Dodger Tait's mob.

'I sat for five minutes with a pistol against my head. Never been so scared in my life. It wasn't Tait so much as the bleedin' driver. If there was a stone in the road he was going out of his way to run over it. Every bump I could feel Tait twitching.'

'Then he made a dash for it . . .'

Bulman nodded. 'A right silly monkey. He must have known he had no chance. The others got caught in the van. I was sitting on top of that spotty-faced youth, whatsisname . . . Lenny Evans. Couldn't move or I'd let him go . . . and it all happened so fast. One minute Tait was scarpering, the next he was being blown ten yards across the bleedin' pavement.'

'Who shot him?' Lucy asked quietly.

'Bloody Dennis Holmes, wasn't it. I mean, there was nothing else he could *do*. Tait had a copper at point blank range. But when Holmes shot he made sure he got the head. He's a nervous shooter, Lucy. He doesn't trust himself to hit a shoulder. I don't like that. I don't like Dennis Holmes.'

Lucy sipped her coffee, her cheerful features darker, now, as Bulman finished the account.

She said, 'But Holmes won't get carpeted . . .?'

Bulman shrugged. 'Tait fired a shot. Holmes was off the hook the moment Tait's finger tightened on the trigger. There'll be an inquiry, an inquest, but if Holmes can live with his conscience, then he's totally in the clear.'

'All's well that ends well,' Lucy said drily.

'Yeah,' Bulman murmured. 'Except that I'll have to go to court as a witness. And bloody Greenstein slipped the net.'

Lucy sighed. 'Back to square one.'

'Not that bad,' Bulman corrected. Lucy was having

a good effect on him; he was already brighter, already shaking off the feeling of failure that had been dogging him since the early morning. 'Square five, maybe. Maybe even square six. Greenstein was driving a burgundy-coloured Bentley when last seen: which was by me, as the police bustled me into their custody. Registration number HKK 951X. Also, it's got an F sticker on the rear left of the boot. The car is registered in the name of Andalusian Holdings with a company office in Holborn.'

Lucy scribbled these facts down on her small notepad. She said, 'A company office from which he has now fled, no doubt. What was he doing in Limehouse?'

'The Maritime Shipping Company are a subsidiary of Andalusian. I followed him there on a hunch.' He sighed. 'I don't get hunches like that more than twice a year. Everything was right: except that Dodger Tait knew that there was a dock payroll in the safe. And the bloody Sweeney knew that Tait knew, and were there in force. And Greenstein slipped through my fingers and is probably back in the States by now.'

Lucy patted his hand. 'Nil desperandum.'

Bulman smiled thinly. 'Quite so. Exceptio probat regulam de rebus non exceptis.'

'Meaning?'

'Meaning there's still a chance he's in London,' Bulman said confidentially.

'But where?'

'Who knows? I'll bell the airlines. See if the bird has flown. You sniff around the posh hotels . . .'

Lucy nodded as she scribbled notes, listing the hotels that immediately sprang to mind. 'And their car parks, of course.'

'Their car parks?'

Lucy looked up and smiled that canny Scots smile that Bulman remembered so well from her father. 'If he's still working the Smoke,' she said, 'He'll still have the Bentley. He's that sort of bloke, by all accounts . . .'

With a grin, and a nod that expressed his admiration,

Bulman said, 'Dead right. Lucinda, you're a great bloke . . .'

By four o'clock in the afternoon, Lucy had checked out all the major Mayfair and Picadilly hotels, and not found a trace of Greenstein. As she called Bulman from the lobby of the London Hilton, she could have wished for no more in life than a year-long bath, and a gentle massage . . . an endless, gentle massage.

Bulman had done the phone circuit of the airlines and had found no booking in the name Greenstein; that meant precious little, of course, since Elias Greenstein could certainly have used one of his several aliases. Bulman had felt the investment of time and effort had been worth it because of one, almost infallible rule of the game: people in a hurry make silly mistakes.

Greenstein was in a hurry. He might well have thought that it was safe to use his own identity to take a flight to the U.S.A.

It was a chance worth taking, and therefore it had been a chance worth George Bulman's taking. But he had come up with nothing.

His sixth sense told him that Greenstein was still in the country.

'Where next, Lucinda?'

'The Intercontinental. Then the Russell. Then Fiona's Massage Parlour. That's not anything to do with Elias Greenstein. That's my reward to myself.'

'I'm not sure that Fiona will know how to handle you,' Bulman said drily. 'But good luck.'

It took Lucy a while to locate the Intercontinental Hotel, nestled in a bleak back street, behind Oxford Circus. It had a ramped entrance to its underground car park and Lucy cautiously walked down into the cool, gloomy subterranean space. She could hear a man humming to himself, and searched among the ranks of gleaming cars for the source of the activity.

The place was a silent repository of wealth – Rolls-

Royces, Bentleys, Jaguars and sleek, low sports cars. She checked the registration of each Bentley, but Greenstein's was not among them.

As she turned back towards the ramped exit, she was startled to see a tall shape standing there, a man whose features at first remained in darkness.

'What's *your* game, lady?' he asked abruptly. 'What're you doing here?'

It was the attendant, she realized. He had a car leather in one hand, and was wearing overalls. A young man, black and leanly handsome, he took several slow steps towards Lucy, but seemed more puzzled by her than threatening towards her.

Lucy smiled her easiest smile and glanced around at the cars. 'I'm looking for a Bentley. Friend of mine's staying in London but I don't know what hotel.'

The attendant cocked his head, the expression on his face one of the most amused disbelief. He seemed to be saying, and all the phones are out of order, eh? But aloud he said, 'Bentleys are ten a penny round here.'

'It's a maroon-coloured job,' Lucy elaborated, watching the young man carefully, trying to sense how far she might push for information, and when he might start becoming suspicious. 'Registration HKK 951X. It's got a French nationality sticker. You know . . . the letter F.'

'I know,' the attendant said drily. 'And it's still a very, very long shot.'

He wiped his hands on the car leather, and seemed to relax a little, walking round Lucy, appraising her quickly.

Lucy said, with a sigh, 'I figured that. I've been round fourteen hotels already today.'

'This friend ain't being too friendly, eh?'

Time for honesty, Lucy said to herself, although she was certain the young man had guessed her game already. 'As a matter of fact,' she said confidentially, 'It's not a friend.'

'Well, *what* a surprise,' the attendant said, unsurprised. 'A private Dick, right?'

With mock horror, Lucy said, 'And I thought I was unique.'

The attendant laughed. 'Ten a penny, girl. Usually at least one a day, creeping round here checking registrations. What is it? Divorce?'

'We don't touch divorce,' Lucy said. 'Dirty business.'

'Repossession, then.'

'Something like that,' Lucy agreed, and handed the attendant a business card, with the Bentley's details scribbled out on the back. 'I'd appreciate a call if you *should* see the vehicle in question.'

'I'm sure you would, girl. I'm sure you would. So let's do the deal, shall we? A pony now . . . and a monkey if I deliver. All right?'

'Nothing doing.'

The attendant shrugged, then smiled. 'Oh. Well, let's hear your counter-proposal.' His eyes sparkled in the dim light, with amusement, Lucy thought. He'd only been trying it on. She pulled two five pound notes from her blouson pocket. 'Ten quid now,' she said, handing them to the man. 'And fifty if you find the Bentley.'

He took the money, folded it carefully, then smiled broadly. 'You drive a desperate hard bargain.'

'How will you know if the vehicle's around?'

'By *phoning* around,' he said. 'In this strange world of half-light and silent cars there's a race of men who all know each other real well. A brotherhood as old as underground car parks themselves.'

Lucy laughed, and said quickly, 'You mean you guys run a car-hire service using clients' motors.'

'What an infamous suggestion,' the young man said in a tone of horror. He moved to polish the headlights of a Silver Shadow, then flashed Lucy his broad grin again. 'You want a lift home?'

*

If George Bulman had been optimistic about Dennis Holmes' chances of coming through the inquiry about the shooting with a clean slate, Dennis Holmes himself felt no such certainty.

He had acted fast – he had *had* to act fast, Tait was shooting a colleague – but he had acted just that fraction *too* fast. He had acted without thinking. That was the difference between himself and so many of his colleagues, the men whose reflexes were as sharp as his, but whose minds could engage the situation just that little more clearly.

With some of Holmes' colleagues, Dodger Tait would still have been alive. Wounded, but alive.

Holmes had no doubts at all that he would be cleared of manslaughter. He would not be retired, or reprimanded, or embarrassed in any way by his own Force. Of course not.

Line of duty. The name of the game.

But the killing would have registered nonetheless. He was a young man, a young copper, and had begun with every ounce of ambition that his friends and colleagues had had. He had watched those who crept up the scale, and those who sank down. He knew how an incident like the Tait shooting could have the same effect upon a man's career as placing a brick wall in front of him.

Holmes would not go up the ladder, now, and he would not go down. He would not go anywhere. Slow death. Nowhere, unless he could somehow make amends. And the thought of how many years he would have to wait for that opportunity to arise was the most depressing thing of all to an ambitious copper like Dennis Holmes.

Strangely, the thought that Dodger Tait might have had friends, and that those friends might have been aggrieved at the manner of Tait's death, had not yet occurred to him.

All that was about to change.

Late in the afternoon of the day of the shooting,

Holmes went to the police mortuary in Willard Street, where Tait's body had been taken. He imagined that all necessary identification had already been made. His job, now, was to fetch Tait's personal effects and take them to forensic, before returning them to the family.

Jim Benson met him at the door. He looked weary, and concerned. As they walked to the check-out counter of the cold, unpleasant building, Benson said, 'So are you suspended, or what?'

'Not yet,' Holmes said. The man behind the counter produced a large polythene bag at Holmes' request: Tait's clothing, and pockets contents. Holmes eyed the gear ruefully. The white shirt was spattered with blood.

He signed for the bag, picked it up and began to walk back to the mortuary's entrance. He hated the smell of disinfectant that always pervaded the air of these places.

'I've had words with Tonto . . .' 'Tonto' was the Metropolitan lower rank's name for Commander Tony Curtis. Curtis had now taken over the number 1 spot in the InterCity Squad, George Bulman's old bunch.

'And he says . . .?'

'I'm to carry on with my normal duties. I'm not to talk to the Press, nor to any of Tait's friends or family. I've had to turn in my shooter, but I'm not being suspended during the inquiry.'

'That's something, anyhow,' Benson said. 'What a bastard. If you hadn't've shot, Ronnie Slater would be a dead man.'

'Probably not,' Holmes said grimly. 'Tait's shooter was only a two-two.'

'You weren't to know that. You couldn't've known that.'

'Oh my God . . .'

Benson glanced at his colleague in puzzlement, then saw the way Holmes was staring along the corridor. At the main entrance, three people were just entering the mortuary. Two were older women, the third a girl, her face tear-stained and red. She was wearing a black coat, and her dyed hair was dishevelled.

'Who is it?' Benson whispered.

'Only bloody Karen Scroop,' Holmes retorted. 'Tait's wife. Bennie Scroop's daughter.'

As Karen Scroop walked along the corridor, Holmes opened the glass partition door that separated them. Karen acknowledged the gesture with the merest nod, and started to go past the two policemen. Holmes held the polythene bag of effects behind his back, hoping that there would be no encounter.

But Karen Scroop suddenly realized where she had seen the two men before, and stopped. She turned to face Holmes, and her watery eyes narrowed. She smiled a thin, angry smile.

'Well, well. Dennis Holmes himself.'

The two women with Karen stared sourly at the policemen, one of them tugging at Karen's sleeve. The girl shook her off and walked slowly up to the man who had killed her husband.

She saw the polythene bag, and smiled even more sourly. 'Even when he's dead you've got to go and test his things. You sick man, Dennis. You sick, sad people.'

'Just routine, Mrs Tait. Letter of the law.'

'How's it feel to have a notch on your gun, Dennis? How's it feel to remember what my Dodger's head looked like after you'd used it for target practice?'

'He shot first, Mrs Tait. He knew the score.'

The girl curled her lip, looked the man up and down. 'Did he, now. He knew the score did he? Two-two against three-eight. Nice, even odds. And now he's cold, and the bastard who killed him is walking off with his clothes, just to make sure that everything, every bit of the book, can be thrown at his *corpse*.'

Holmes felt his face flushing and glanced uncomfortably at Jim Benson, who remained impassively stony, staring at the woman.

Holmes said, 'Mrs Tait, there's nothing I can say. Except to offer my sympathies. All right?'

For a moment she said nothing. She just stared at D.I. Dennis Holmes, and the look in her eyes was almost pity. Then she shook her head and stepped right up to him. 'Sympathy? It's not sympathy I'm after, Dennis. Oh no.' Holmes stiffened but held his ground as she took his arm and pulled him slightly down, so that she could whisper in his ear.

'Dennis, it's got to be done. You took my husband's life. You left his kid without a father. You're the bloke what's broken my heart. And we're taking you, Del boy. Taking you in exchange. The word's out. Everyone knows what it is I want brought to me in a brown paper bag. So make your peace, Del. You ain't got much time . . .'

Holmes felt his legs shaking, but he straightened up as Karen Scroop took a step away from him. Her words, whispered so urgently, so confidentially in his ear, made him feel sick as he let them echo. The smell of disinfectant in the mortuary almost overwhelmed him.

Too shaken to speak, he was too slow to see the change in Karen Scroop's face, the look of animal fury that suddenly chased away her expression of benign pity.

She screamed so suddenly that it made both Holmes and Benson jump.

'Murderer!'

And as the word reverberated in the cold corridor, she slashed out with her right hand, and her nails raked his flesh, laying his cheek open. Holmes screamed and struck her hand away, clutching at the torn skin, feeling blood pour through his fingers.

In this way he stood, Benson holding him, watching as Karen Scroop laughed at him, listening to her laughter as the two women pulled her away, deeper into the building, to where her husband's body was waiting for her.

Chapter Three

George Bulman was up early the following morning, but not to get out on the street again: the Greenstein case had put him well behind with his other professional activity. Four small clocks sat on his work bench, their innards half displayed, waiting for gentle hands to make them right again.

Tired though he was, Bulman loved clocks so much that he had been unable to sleep for thinking about what he needed to do to them. A steaming mug of tea by his right elbow, he worked contentedly during the early hours of morning, letting his concern for yesterday's events fade away.

Elias Greenstein, in particular, he pushed to the back of his mind.

Then, at nine o'clock – and just as he put the finishing touches to a small, brass lantern clock, which began to tick loudly and happily again – the phone rang.

He sighed, pulled back from the work bench and walked through to the office, to Lucy's desk, where her notepad was open, ready for messages. He rummaged for a pencil, then answered the phone. 'S.T.G. Investigations.'

A voice, hushed and conspiratorial, said, 'Hey, man, I got this number for a chick called Lucy . . .'

'She's not here right now,' Bulman said patiently. 'Can I help? I happen to be her *boss*.' He emphasized the word slightly, suspecting that Lucy might have chosen not to explain that she worked *for* somebody.

The man on the phone hesitated, then said, 'Okay. Here's the message . . .' Bulman wrote as the man spoke. 'The red Bentley is in the car wash.'

'The red . . . Bentley . . . is in . . .'

Murmuring aloud as he scribbled on the pad, Bulman suddenly realized what he was writing.

Greenstein's Bentley!

'Where? What car wash? Who're you?'

'Alderney Street. Listen, we've got him trapped, but hurry, man, we can't keep him there for ever.'

'We're on our way,' Bulman said, and emitted a little cry of gleeful triumph.

Lucy was just arriving at the office. She looked bright and cheery, clutching two carrier bags of food supplies, but her smile vanished as she saw Bulman running towards her through the office.

'Morning, Lucinda. Come on . . .'

'Where's the fire?'

'In a car wash.'

'A car wash?'

'The Bentley! Greenstein's Bentley. In a car wash. Your snout phoned up.'

'Great!'

Delightedly, Lucy stacked the bags just inside the door and quickly followed Bulman out onto the street again. Her small car, a now-cream 2CV, only just big enough to take the two of them, was parked close by.

'I'll drive,' Bulman said, but Lucy was having none of it. She unlocked the driver's door and hopped nimbly into the seat. 'My snout. My car. I'll do the driving,' she said. 'You know the rules.'

Grumbling, Bulman climbed into the passenger seat. He belted himself in, then crossed himself. Lucy ignored him.

It took fifteen minutes to reach Alderney Street. Lucy drove fast, weaving in and out of the traffic, and hopping red lights whenever it appeared to be safe. Bulman hung on for dear life, keeping his eyes keen for police.

As they pulled into the forecourt of the garage, the first thing Bulman saw was the car wash operating. It was stuck, or appeared to be . . . the great blue washing rollers were stationary by the doors of the car that sat among them. The rollers span, and water poured, but nothing was moving either forwards or backwards.

'Nice job,' he said to the young man who came running towards them. Lucy greeted the same youth. Two other men stood, apprehensive yet smiling, watching the 'broken' car wash. They all wore overalls.

'This place is run by Luther,' the young man said. 'He called me a few minutes ago. I came as fast as I could . . .'

Lucy glanced round and saw the Silver Shadow parked at the side of the garage. The attendant caught the glance and grinned. 'Gotta keep the engine turned over.'

'Well done,' she said. They walked to the others.

'But you'd better have a righteous good explanation for keeping him inside that thing for twenty-nine minutes, man. He's gonna be real aggravated.'

Bulman smiled. 'His aggravation don't matter. Lucy? Drive the CV across the exit. Block him. When she's done that,' he said to the attendant. 'Turn the water off and watch the man run like a snared rat . . .'

One of the other garage men drove a beaten-up Bedford van, its sides daubed with Rasta images, across the rear of the car wash. When Lucy was in position, Bulman grinned, then gave the thumbs up.

'At last,' he murmured to himself, and stepped towards the spinning rollers.

Everything slowed, then stopped. The sound of rushing water died abruptly. Machinery creaked and clicked. The roller arms swung away from the car. The red Bentley gleamed, water dripping from its sills.

Bulman stroke quickly over and wrenched the driver's door open to confront Greenstein. 'You're a tricky ponce, Elias,' he roared, 'but there's no escape from . . .'

He didn't complete the sentence. Internally he appended the words, 'Oh Good God Almighty. What the hell have we done?'

A chubby, balding man sat behind the wheel of the

car, his face white as death, his eyes wide with apprehension. He stared at Bulman, and jumped with every movement that Bulman made.

'My name's not Elias, it's Anthony,' he said. 'Is there some problem?'

'Bloody underground car parks!' George Bulman muttered, as he came back from the bar of the Green Man with two Scotches. He placed them on the corner table, where Lucy McGinty sat looking up at him. She smiled and shrugged slightly.

'Anyone can make a mistake, George.'

Bulman grumbled as he undid his jacket. He grumbled as he raised the glass to his lips. He drained off the Scotch, placed the glass on the table, staring at it.

And grumbled.

Lucy watched him, knowing that behind the gruff façade he was probably thinking very hard about what might have gone wrong. She waited her moment, bided her time . . .

'Anyway,' she said. 'He was very good about it. The new owner. He could have cut up very rough.'

'He was water-shocked. He'd just been imprisoned in a car wash for thirty minutes. Not even Game for a Laugh does that to you. Just as he thinks he's safe some gorilla opens the door and shouts at him that he's a ponce. The man was shocked. Stunned. As am I.'

Bulman raised his empty glass and stared at the light through its coarsely cut facets.

Lucy tipped some of her own whisky into the empty vessel and said, 'Anyway, while you were sweet-talking him, I went through the glove compartment.'

'I should hope so,' Bulman grumbled. But he relaxed slightly and watched his associate. Waiting. From Lucy's expression he would have known that she'd discovered something of value.

'Anybody can make a mistake,' Lucy repeated, and Bulman smiled.

'You didn't make a mistake, Lucinda. That was a good tip.'

'Well *thank you*. I'll buy the next round for that.' She leaned forward first, though, and pulled a scrap of paper from her pocket. She'd scrawled words on it when the podgy owner of the Bentley had been transfixed by Bulman's apologetic patter.

'Innocent chummy is Anthony Ashton. He pays a man called Lawrence Culpepper twenty-one thousand for the motor.' She frowned and looked up. 'Twenty-one thousand! That's a lot of shampoo.'

'Get on with it . . . what else?'

'He paid it through a car leasing company called Four Wheel Banking. The Bentley's log book and papers are in the name of Andalusian Holdings.'

'Lawrence Culpepper by another name,' Bulman mused.

'Has to be Greenstein by *two* other names,' Lucy finished. 'Greenstein, Culpepper, Andalusian. A typical Greenstein set-up.'

'Could be an associate,' Bulman speculated. 'Greenstein doesn't tend to use aliases.'

'Perhaps . . .'

He grinned at Lucy. 'Oh how sweet the dawn that spreads its light around. How sweet to be alive and six feet overground!'

Lucy chuckled as she sipped the remains of her Scotch and watched George Bulman return to his normal state of cheer. 'Who wrote that?'

'I did.'

'I thought as much. So what happens now, George? I imagine we check the leasing company and find out where they paid the money to.'

'We'll make a detective out of you yet, girl.'

Lucy stood up, ready for action.

Bulman held out his glass to her. 'I'll take a double.'

While Lucy did some phone work, Bulman tinkered with one of the nicest clocks he had so far been offered for repair. It was a Jeremy Martin, made in Bath in 1860. The casing was well maintained, but the mechanism itself had failed because of corrosion. The clock had been brought in by a local collector, a wealthy writer living along the Roman Road. Bulman knew for a fact that the man had over two thousand clocks.

It was an account he valued. It was an account that might, yet, see one retired D.I. basking in the sun of the Caribbean.

He could hear Lucy, out the front in the office, murmuring in reasonably urgent tones. She was persuading somebody to part with information. Lucy had many phone voices, but her persuasion voice was the most dramatic and the most effective.

It was while he half listened to her voice, and half romanced about the possibility of renovating two thousand clocks, a single order, five years' work, paid for in advance, that his knee began to hurt.

Like most people, George Bulman had two knees. Morphogenetically they were identical. Anatomically they were indistinguishable. Physiologically they appeared to be perfectly normal. But Bulman's right knee had a quirk that was quite undetectable by ordinary medical means: it could warn him of trouble.

As he worked on the clock he began to feel uneasy. Something nasty was brewing up, something that was neither Elias Greenstein, nor Lucy McGinty's tea (which was still, despite repeated lessons, among the nastiest things that Bulman had to regularly encounter).

He sat back and let the discomfort rattle him. He was working on no case but the Greenstein case, and that was simply the case of a slick con-man not yet quite finished conning. The blagging of yesterday, despite Tait's death, was routine, as much as such tragedies could ever be so classified . . .

Something was about to break. An ill-wind blowing . . .

Lucy broke through his sudden train of thought, his

briefly felt tension. She came into the back room and leaned over the work-bench.

'What've you got?' Bulman asked.

'Not sure. Four Wheel Banking paid for the Bentley by bank transfer. But not to Lawrence Culpepper. They paid the twenty-one grand to a firm called Park Lane Autos.'

Bulman thought about that. He removed his jeweller's spectacles and stared absently at Lucy.

On the bench, the Jeremy Martin chimed delicately.

'Sounds as if he's bought a new car. Traded in the Bentley for a second motor.'

'Good reasoning,' Lucy said.

'It's encouraging at least,' Bulman corrected. 'What it means is this. If Greenstein isn't using an alias, and using aliases isn't part of his modus operandum, then, if he *has* bought a new car, it would imply that he's still in the smoke. And we can still nab the bugger.'

Lucy straightened up, pursing her lips as she thought it all through. Then she grimaced, shrugged, and smiled. 'I'm confused. But if you say so, it sounds great . . .'

Now George Bulman exercised a moment's caution. He raised a finger, a gesture of wariness.

'Not necessarily . . .'

His damned knee *still* ached. But it wouldn't play up just because of a con-artist like Greenstein. What the hell was it trying to tell him?

'Not necessarily. Those whom the Gods wish to destroy, they first present with an obvious clue. Let's not get caught out, girl.'

Lucy muttered, 'You're still smarting over the car wash incident.'

'Made a right bloody idiot of myself,' Bulman said, confirming that embarrassment *was* a part of his caution.

'Let me ask you a question, boss. How much do we make if we catch Elias G.?'

Looking up at her, Bulman frowned. 'It depends. A

percentage of what we recover from him gets paid to us. Could be fifteen, twenty grand. Why?'

'I was just thinking that for fifteen grand I'd trap a double-decker *bus* load of Anthony Ashtons in a car wash. I'd suggest that it's time you stopped worrying about the moments when things go wrong and concentrate on the moments when things go right.'

Bulman stared at her, slightly shocked, slightly amused. He said . . . after a moment . . . 'You're right, Lucy. You're damned right, and I'm a damned fool. Go and make some tea. And I'll concentrate on the good moments before and after drinking it!'

'Wretch!' she declared, and, looking around for some way to punish him, stuck his pencil, eraser side down, into the scummy remains of his mid-day cuppa, still lingering in a large china mug at the edge of his workbench.

'Anyway,' she said, placing a scrap of notepaper in front of him. 'There it is. Park Lane Autos. What happens now? Apart from me *not* making you tea?'

'You repeat your favourite job,' Bulman said with a thin smile. 'You know, go around the posh hotels. Porters, reception, car parks, although I hesitate to include them. You know the score, Lucy. Take a photo of the man from the file, just in case he is calling himself by an alias. But go softly. Very softly. Any hint of a posse and he'll be off out of the country. All right?'

With a sigh that indicated her joy at the prospect of another day's trudging the streets of Central London, Lucy nodded. 'Okay. But won't *you* have scared him off? He knows there's a P.I. after him now. And that little incident yesterday must have warned him off . . .'

'I don't think so. He's clever, is our Elias. A bit too clever maybe. He'll see yesterday as a triumph for his luck, not a warning as to his imminent danger. He'll feed on that luck. It's called arrogance. He's high, now, high on success, high on confidence. That's when mistakes get made. Like this car sale. So the hotels are worth a look, Lucinda. Our man isn't the sort of monkey who'll check into a cheap Kensington flea-pit for a few nights.'

His knee gave him a twinge. He rubbed it, frowning. The Jeremy Martin kept ticking, a good job well done. Lucy resigned herself to her task . . .

Then the phone began to ring.

Bulman stared through into the front of the shop. Waiting.

Lucy said, 'Are you going to get that or shall I?'

'You get it,' he said.

She walked through to the front and lifted the receiver. A moment later she called, 'It's for you.'

'Who is it?' he whispered, but she just shrugged and placed the receiver down on his P.I.'s desk. He walked through to the office, wiping his hands – which were oily – on his apron. '*Who* is it?' he asked Lucy again. She had sat down at her own desk and was thumbing through the phone book. Now she realized that Bulman was disturbed by something and she frowned, shaking her head.

'He said it was personal. Sorry, George . . . should I have asked?'

He picked up the phone. A moment later he exhaled noisily, and irritably, and glanced at Lucy with an expression of total exasperation.

'Hello, Dennis. Listen, Dennis, it's after hours, and I'm busy . . . No, Dennis . . . now listen, if you want a statement I'll give it to you in the morning. I'm *busy*. And I didn't see the blagging, and I didn't really witness the shooting, and I've got bruises on both arms from the courteous arrest by that ponce rozzer chummy of yours, Benson . . .'

There was a moment's pause and Bulman frowned, looking at Lucy, yet not looking at her. She could sense the change in him, the sudden realization that the call from the policeman was not an official call.

'Why would you want to see me on *personal* business, Dennis?' Bulman asked. Whatever Holmes said it must have been agitated because Bulman began to make calming gestures to the phone itself. 'Okay, okay. I'll meet you in half an hour. Can you get up to the Shanghai Road? Go to the Battle of Hastings, it's a nice quiet, select boozer. Yeah. See you there.'

'Dennis Holmes?' Lucy said as he placed the receiver back. Bulman nodded confirmation, but he was puzzled by the content of the call.

'He's the skipper of the team that nicked me yesterday.'

'I know. What'd he want?'

'Nothing to do with the job, he said. A personal chat, but to do with business. He sounded worried. I don't like the bloke, but my equivalent of the Hippocratic oath makes it impossible to turn down a voice in trouble.'

'Maybe his clocks have stopped,' Lucy said wryly.

'From his voice,' Bulman retorted, 'I think he's worried about more than his clocks . . .'

With a shrug, Lucy said, 'I'll get on with the Greenstein enquiry. Leave you to your social drinking.'

'Uh-uh. You're coming with me. Get a coat.'

As he spoke, Bulman stripped off his oily apron and shrugged on his heavy leather jacket.

'Why?'

'Witness.'

'You're getting paranoid, George Bulman,' Lucy said as she pulled on her own jacket.

'Too bloody true.'

They walked down to the Battle of Hastings, found a corner table and enjoyed a quiet drink together. Holmes didn't turn up for forty minutes, and he looked pale and harassed as he came over to them, the right side of his face covered with plaster. He was wearing a black donkey jacket and faded denims, the appearance of a man who – in a profession like Holmes' – was trying to throw off his natural identity.

'How's business, George?' Holmes asked.

Bulman said, 'I mind it.'

'Very funny.' The policeman shuffled uneasily, looking between Bulman and Lucy as if unsure whether to sit down or not. 'Plenty of punters?'

'Body-and-soul-together level, Dennis. You know how it is in the world of the private Dick, harassed on the street, ignored by his old police chums . . . When he's not being arrested by them, that is.'

Holmes grinned sheepishly. 'Stupid mistake. Sorry, George.'

After a strained moment's silence, Bulman said tetchily, 'Well don't just stand there, Dennis. Fetch us a drink. A large Scotch. Each.'

'Yeah. Of course. Won't be a moment.'

When he returned with the drinks he unbuttoned his coat and sat down. He drained most of his own whisky in one gulp, and his face reddened slightly behind the dark stubble of his beard.

Bulman let him find his own level, let him choose the moment to talk. At last Holmes said, 'How many times have you had the word put on your life, George? As a jobbing copper, I mean?'

So that's it! The word's on the poor bastard. Killing Tait has tolled a death knell . . .

'Depends what you mean,' Bulman said carefully, aware of how shaky the policeman was, how close to the edge. 'If you mean threats that might have been carried out on a dark night, when I might have been drunk and just fallen into the monkey's path, with a convenient wrench lying around . . . hundreds. If you mean *serious* word . . .'

'That's just what I mean.'

'Five,' Bulman said. 'Five moments where I felt serious concern, and had to get the protection side of the Department oiled and standing by.'

Holmes murmured, 'But they didn't come to anything.'

'Not unless my doctor's short sighted or been lying to me.'

'Did they make you feel sick?'

'Sick as a pig. But not the threats themselves. You

get taken off the street, and that made me mad. How about you, Dennis? How many times has the word been put out on you?'

Holmes drained his glass, and toyed with it, resting it lightly on the table. 'Two. Two serious threats.'

Bulman said, 'But number three has really got you rattled.'

'I'll get some more drinks,' Lucy said. Holmes smiled wanly at her as she got up from the table, and as she vanished towards the bar he looked hard at Bulman.

'Number three, George, is trouble like I never thought to *know* about.'

'Tell me about it. In detail. That is, if you want to.'

Holmes nodded. 'It's Karen Scroop, right? Karen Tait. You know, Dodger's old lady. She come down the body shop. I didn't expect to see her there. Caught me by surprise. There I was, worried about me bleedin' pension, and she comes in, calm as you like, and has a little word with me.'

'A little word about getting your affairs in order.'

'She's going to top me. Not her, of course. But she's going to have it done . . .'

Bulman smiled, and his attempt at lightening Holmes' mood went wrong as he said, 'You didn't expect her to invite you to the Scroop and Kray Christmas party, did you?'

Holmes looked ashen-faced and angry. After a moment Bulman muttered his apology, adding, 'So what'd she say? Karen . . .'

Dennis Holmes tentatively touched the plaster on his cheek. 'She whispered it like an apology. Dennis, she says, it's got to be done. You took my husband's life. And we're taking you. She said the word was out and that I should make my peace.' He shuddered slightly, staring at the table top. 'Then she stepped back and sort of smiled. Like she was sad. Then she ripped my face open and screamed "murderer".'

Bulman said, 'She was hysterical. People can behave in a very scary way when they're hysterical.'

'She'll do it,' Holmes said urgently. 'She'll get it done. Her family's close, and they all love her. They'll do anything for her.'

With a shake of his head Bulman murmured, 'Bennie Scroop's too wise. He won't allow a copper to be topped. Not even for his daughter.'

His face darkening, Holmes smiled thinly, almost exasperated. 'Then, George . . . you don't know about the Honour of the Villain. Bennie Scroop is retired from the game. All he has that he really enjoys, now, is his family. When a bloke like Bennie goes in off the streets he gets romantic ideas about defending honour, eye for an eye stuff, Mafiosa stuff. I've seen it happen, George. You too. Come on.'

Bulman stared at the policeman, at the earnest worry in his eyes, the slight trembling of his lips. Holmes was right *and* he was wrong. Sure, Bennie Scroop was an old man who now fancied himself as a 'godfather' figure. But Bennie hadn't liked Dodger Tait, his son-in-law, and anyway, he was clever enough to know that if Holmes *was* killed then a great deal of unwelcome police attention would be paid to the Scroop family, and ultimately that could only be the worse for Karen . . .

Karen herself was the problem. Karen had influence. Karen had passion. Karen Scroop would carry hate for years, and that was time enough to find some up-and-coming punk to help her out . . .

He said to Holmes, 'You told your guvnor yet?'

Dennis Holmes just laughed. It was a sound without humour. 'Par for the course, isn't it? The Met's not going to double the guard each time an arresting officer gets cautioned by the Scroops.'

'But you told him.'

'All he offered was a holiday with pay for three or four weeks. A nice little break from routine. Get off the streets for a few days. It's called a temporary suspension pending inquiries . . .' Holmes shrugged. 'I said no.'

'Why?'

'Too easy for them to keep extending the suspension. Might end up working traffic in Tintagel.'

'Think of all that lovely cider,' Bulman said with a smile. And Holmes smiled too. Lucy came back with three glasses of whisky and placed them on the table. Holmes nodded his thanks then said to George Bulman, 'I love it on the streets. Been on the streets for fourteen years now. Been knifed twice. Shot once. Small commendation. It's my job, George, and I love it. But you're only as good as your mind, and your bottle. And you know what worries me now? The way I feel about this whole business, the shaking, the panic . . . George, I reckon I'm *losing* my bottle. And that's a bigger killer than Karen Scroop herself!'

They drank in silence for a minute or two, Lucy keeping discreetly quiet, Bulman waiting for Holmes to make his play . . . and wondering what to do when the policeman *did* come out with what he really wanted.

Holmes was hesitating, that much was clear, so Bulman decided to force the issue.

'Wish I could help you more, mate,' he said, and drained his glass.

Holmes leaned forward. 'George. I'd like to hire you.'

'We're not into protection, Den. Advice I can help you with. Sure. Come round my gaff if you like and we'll talk all night over a nice bottle of malt . . .'

With an abrupt shake of his head, a gesture that came very close to petulance, Holmes said, 'I don't want that, George. I want to find what she's up to. Who she's using. Then I'll nick her for bleedin' conspiracy.'

With an uncomfortable glance at Lucy, Bulman said, 'I have to tell you, Dennis, that it all sounds a bit "iffy". Anyway, I've got a case. I wouldn't have had if your Mr Benson hadn't confused me with a punching bag, and let my own man get away . . .'

To his astonishment Lucy said, brightly, 'Why don't

I take it? You can handle Greenstein, I'll get some street experience.'

Holmes stared at her, slowly shaking his head in disbelief.

Lucy said, 'I mean . . . we help you out now, Dennis. You can help us in the future, right?'

'It's a touch rough for a bird, love,' Holmes said, and the smile vanished from Lucy's face.

'I thought it was a bird we were discussing. *Love,*' she said angrily.

Holmes looked uncomfortable. To Bulman he said, 'I've heard good things about you two. You've got a few under your belt. Jack Lambie was most impressed . . .'

'Lambie? Impressed?'

'Sure. And Lambie's a good man. Okay. I'll pay the rate. Do it straight. Why should my case be any different from anyone else's? We keep it private and personal. While *you're* on the case, I'm *off* the case. When you're done, we swap roles. No interference. How about it?'

Lucy looked at Bulman hard. 'George . . .?' she said. For some reason she really wanted this case. Adventure, perhaps. Get away from greasy con-men and into some real, hard street action.

'Okay,' Bulman said. 'If that's what you want, you've got it. And it'll cost you two fifty a week, and that doesn't include expenses.'

Holmes shrugged. *No matter.* And he said, 'And you'll keep a watching brief . . .'

'All we can do is find out if she means it. With some hard evidence of intent, it's straight over to the boys in blue.'

'Sounds fair.'

Turning to Lucy, Bulman began to button up his jacket. 'Okay, sleuth, get the details. I'm going to have a crack at my Jeremy Martin again.'

Holmes frowned. 'Who's that? A villain?'

'A clock,' Bulman said. 'But don't worry, Den. We've got some villains on our books too.'

He rose to go. Holmes hesitantly shook hands. 'If there's anything I can do, George. Central Records access, computers, asking around . . .'

'No thanks, Dennis. We've got a system all our own.'

Lucy glanced at him, frowning. *We have? Since when?*

Holmes watched Bulman depart, then turned to Lucy and smiled. 'That's our George. Independent to the back teeth.'

Lucy flipped open her notebook. 'Let's get to work.'

Chapter Four

He had come back to London the moment he'd heard the news. Family affairs, as far as Bennie Scroop were concerned, were more important than anything, even business as delicate as the business that had taken him to Glasgow. It was legitimate business, of course – buying and selling whisky liqueurs without the involvement of the usual middle-men – but Scroop, having been on the wrong side of the tracks for so long, could not bear to conduct business *too* openly. So it had taken a day or more for the news of his son-in-law's death to find him.

The meeting of the two Families had immediately broken up. Scroop had driven south during the day, and he arrived outside his daughter's small, east London terraced house at five in the afternoon.

Karen's minder slipped into the sleek black car and nodded greetings to Bennie Scroop.

'She's more angry than upset.'

'She would be. She's a Scroop. Tears later. Justice first.'

'Wants revenge,' the young man said. 'The copper's head on a plate.'

Scroop laughed sourly. 'At least she's been reading her bible.'

There was a minute of silence. Scroop stared out the window at the brightly painted house. Karen and her kid were inside, and Queenie too. He and Queenie had bought the house for their daughter when she'd got married. They'd had to. Tait was a wild boy, ambitious but moneyless. There was no accounting for taste, and in Bennie Scroop's world what someone wanted to do was their business, and he'd go along with their decision. When Karen had fallen for Dodger he'd felt sick at heart; but it was Karen's heart that had mattered to him and he had done his best for the couple.

A car; a house; a loan; and perhaps most of all, letting Tait get away with some of the aggravation he gave his wife.

Karen loved him, even when he was drunk . . .

Bennie Scroop had watched carefully, and set a certain bound over which not even his daughter's husband would step. But Tait had kept his respect for his family, and had even tried to join the Scroop 'firm'.

That was a decision that had been all Bennie Scroop's. And the decision was no.

You're too wild, kid. You ought to get legitimate. You're mucking about with more lives than your own . . .

Bennie Scroop had not liked his son-in-law. A part of the old man could feel only relief, now. It was a part he kept subdued because his daughter was grieving, and he would not have wished that on the girl, not even for the parting of Dodger Tait from his earthly toil.

'Better go in.'

Scroop got out of the car and straightened the jacket of his dark business suit. As he crossed the road he tightened his tie, checked his cuffs. He might have been any City gent, any respectable businessman from the bank. But the look of his hair, the premature silvering despite the thickness of it, gave the final lie to his appearance.

He had the look, and the mark, of a man who had spent more than half his life in prison.

Queenie met him at the door. She smiled wanly, holding her cigarette to one side as she turned her face for her husband's perfunctory kiss. She was a handsome woman, her hair dyed platinum, her figure still full.

'Handle her carefully, Bennie. She's on the edge.'

'Don't worry, Queenie. Make us some tea, eh?'

He stepped through into the small living room and

stood by the door, watching his grandson as the toddler staggered across the deep carpet in his baby walker. He looked happy, unaffected by the mood of gloom that pervaded the rest of the house. The living room had two black squares of silk covering the mirrors, but apart from that it was as Bennie remembered it: a clutter of photographs on the mantelpiece, flower vases, a TV, a cheap settee and two display cabinets of souvenirs from Spain and Greece.

Karen Scroop stood in the middle of the room, dressed in black, her hair hanging loose around her shoulders. She'd been crying, and she was smoking. The ash-tray was full to overflowing.

'Hello, love.'

'Hello, Dad.'

Father and daughter stared at each other, sadness and discomfort making them shuffle for a moment.

Then Karen looked down, put a hand to her eyes and started to sob.

Bennie Scroop took two quick steps towards her and hugged her tightly, patting her gently on the back.

There had been few times in his long life when Bennie Scroop had been seriously concerned that things, relating to his family, were about to go very, very wrong. To be caught for a job, to be banged away behind bars, to receive threats from other Manors . . . these were occupational hazards, and Scroop had always taken them in his stride. Family rows, bust-ups, these were part of life. The Scroop family was big, violent, independent . . . but Bennie Scroop had held it together by using iron rule tempered with respect for feelings.

He had hardly ever felt real apprehension for the well-being of the family he loved.

Now, though, was one of those times.

He drove to the Dauphin Sporting Club, a small, seedy-looking building in Whitechapel. It was one of several such clubs that Scroop shared ownership of, and was run by one of his most dependable associates: Horse Cromwell.

Inside, the Dauphin was a different world to the scruffy, run-down and dark environment in which it lurked. A well-stocked bar ran down one side of a large gaming area; bright lights illuminated the tables, where croupiers – mostly young, glamorous women – were practising deals and play, and laughing as they idled away the hours until opening.

Scroop stood at the entrance for a moment and surveyed the place. It was only the second time he'd seen the newly refurbished club and he was impressed. Horse had done well. To look at Horse Cromwell was not to think: *taste*. He did not give the appearance of knowing much about fine art decor, or new mode furnishings. Appearance gave the lie.

Cromwell was in his middle fifties, a stocky, muscular man meticulously and fashionably dressed to meet his punters. He had done time in Maidstone with Bennie Scroop, and Scroop found it hard to connect this elegant, if hard-faced man – who looked so youthful with his dyed dark hair – with the greying shadow that had, just four years ago, whispered goodbye from the concrete cemetery in Kent.

Horse Cromwell moved away from the pretty croupier to whom he'd been chatting, clearly giving her encouragement for what might have been her first night on the table, and came over to Scroop. They didn't shake hands.

'How's she taking it, Bennie?'

'Blames me,' Bennie Scroop said, his voice a hoarse whisper. They moved over to the bar and Horse signalled for two drinks, two small gins.

'That's not fair. The bloke was an independent, went on the blagging on his own initiative. Why would she blame you?'

Scroop shrugged. It had been a hard afternoon. Karen had been angry, then upset, then angry again, and he and Queenie had sat with her, letting all the feelings, all the emotions bubble out. If it had been good for Karen to get the things said that she'd said, then Bennie Scroop was happy enough to have been his daughter's punching bag for a few hours.

It was this other thing . . . this damned obsession . . .

He said, 'She blames me because – she says – we ought to have found Tait a place in the Firm.' He sipped the neat gin. 'I thought about it. I've been thinking about it for years. If I'd thought he would've fit, he'd have been in. You know that, Horse.'

Horse Cromwell shrugged, fixing Scroop with his hard, straight stare. One thing about Horse, he'd speak his mind. He'd give it to you straight. He wouldn't hold back on a criticism, even to the man he worked for.

'Maybe you should've. This *is* a family business, Bennie. The important thing about family is you look after them . . .'

'I've always looked after Karen. She's never wanted for a thing.'

Horse said, 'Too much focus on Karen herself, not enough on the fact that Karen and Dodger were a *team*. They were family, Dodger *became* family. I've always felt you shouldn't have left him out in the cold.'

Scroop sniffed dismissively, shaking his head. But he didn't meet Horse's gaze as he said, 'Trouble with Tait . . . he was wild. You know what I mean, Horse. He had no control. He couldn't have blagged a sweet-shop . . . and he wouldn't have fit. It was a hard decision to make. But I made it. I'd have found him some legit work, you know that. But he wanted the Firm. And that wasn't on, Horse. And it breaks my heart that Karen blames me.'

Horse nodded, then slapped Scroop on the arm. 'She'll see the light soon enough, Bennie. Sensible girl, your Karen. As long as she's all right now.'

'That's what worries me. I don't think she is. You know what she wants?'

'What?'

Scroop turned and looked at his friend. 'She only wants me to have the copper that done it terminated.'

For a second, Horse was too surprised to speak. Then he laughed. Then he frowned and quickly shook his head. 'That's crazy talk. She doesn't mean it, Bennie. It's the grief.'

'That's what I said to her. I told her straight. Poor Dodger got croaked in the normal course of his work. Nobody asked him to set up as an armed bleedin' robber, right?'

'Right.'

'And nobody told him it was a good idea to take pot shots at a copper. That tends to result in fatalities. Right?'

'Dead right, Bennie.'

Scroop's expression was grim and he patted his right hand gently on the bar counter, a gesture that clearly indicated the strain he was feeling. 'But she won't listen. She don't see reason. Her Dodger got topped by a trigger-happy copper called Holmes. She ain't going to relax until Holmes is on the slab, with his hands crossed on his chest.'

Horse Cromwell was at a loss for words. He could understand the situation, he could understand Scroop's worry, he could understand Karen's grief. There was nothing to be done until a few days had passed, and time had effected its own brand of healing.

'She'll come round, Bennie. After the funeral.'

The funeral was the next day. It would be a big affair. Scroop had offered to pay for the reception, which would be held in one of his clubs further east. Out of respect for Karen there would be a lot of people at the graveside who would not normally have given Tait the time of day.

'Yeah,' Scroop said. Then he got round to the real reason for his visit, now that Horse was relaxed, softened up. 'Thing is, Horse . . . she's going to need some special looking after.'

'She's got a minder.'

Scroop straightened up and looked at his old friend. 'Yeah. But a minder's just there for physical protection. I mean she needs *special* looking after. Someone she trusts. Someone she can talk to. Someone who can talk to her about how stupid she's being, without her going hysterical.'

Horse Cromwell nodded, agreeing the point. Then he saw the way Scroop was staring at him, a canny, deliberate look.

'Me?'

'I was thinking of you because firstly I trust you like a brother. And secondly, Karen likes you a lot too. And you like Karen, if I'm not much mistaken.'

'Ever since she was a nipper,' Horse agreed. 'But I don't—'

Scroop silenced him with a gentle pressure on his arm, and a smile that might have been the smile of equals. 'There's only you, Horse. It's got to be you. Stick with her, be her pal. Talk to her. Take no nonsense. A few days, like you said, and she'll be through the worst.'

'I dunno, boss . . .'

'It would make me feel totally relaxed to know you was escorting my Karen about, looking after her. Do it for me, Horse. I may be a hard bastard, but right now I need your help badly. I don't want my little girl to end up slammed away for conspiracy to murder.'

That got him. Horse Cromwell went noticeably pale. He nodded grimly, then stuck out his hand. The handshake was the silent sealing of a bond.

The following morning the body of Edward 'Dodger' Tait was lowered into the earth. It was an overcast day, but still, not a breath of wind. The priest's words drifted to the edge of the cemetery, where two people watched the ceremony from afar.

Karen stood at the grave's edge, silent and composed, her arm linked through her father's. She shed no tears, made no sound, but her gaze never left the coffin. Only when the lid, with its fine brass plaque, was deeper in the soil than the light could penetrate did she turn away, staring into the middle distance. The rest of the funeral party waited, hands folded in front of them, waited for the widow to leave. She looked at them all, recognizing many faces, not recognizing others. The faces were hard, the cut of the clothes sharp, the solemn expressions more a reflection of personality than grief. She knew full well that most of the people who had come to see Tait to his last resting place were there because of her father, and for no other reason.

'So that's that,' she said quietly, and walked slowly with her father back towards the black limousine that led the cortege. 'End of a dream.'

'You're still young,' Bennie said. He patted her hand. 'You're a beautiful young girl, Karen, and there'll be someone else along for you. Mark my words.'

They walked with stiff dignity, listening to the shuffling of the others behind. Horse Cromwell was very close, his gaze fixed on the girl.

'I loved him, Daddy. I loved Ted. You don't seem to realize that.'

'I do. I do know that.'

'There can't be any others.' She looked up at her father and her gaze hardened, a searching stare that challenged Bennie Scroop directly. 'Not until it's done. Not until my Dodger's been revenged.'

He smiled at her, though behind the smile he was experiencing an anxiety that was almost alien to him.

'It's out of the question, love. You've got a life to live, with your kid, with whoever happens along. You go conspiring to kill coppers, what sort of life do you think the boy will have?'

Clumsy, he thought. But maybe that's the way through. Can't appeal to her herself, so appeal to her motherhood . . .

Karen looked grim for a moment. 'Dad,' she said softly, 'I never asked you for anything before. I know you've been good to me, generous, to me and Dodger . . . but I never *asked* for anything. Never.'

Scroop smiled thinly and squeezed her arm. 'I know, love. And I know what it is you're saying, and feeling. But topping a copper is out of the question. It's suicide, Karen. And because I know *you*, I know you won't ask it of me.' He looked at her as he spoke this last, and her pale features were staring grimly ahead.

But she nodded and smiled. 'You're right, Dad. I wouldn't ask you. I just miss my Dodger, that's all . . .'

'I know you do, sweetheart. Good girl.' More parental patting and reassurance. 'Things are going to be okay. You've been a brave girl.'

'Not much bleedin' option,' Karen said, but there was a hint of affection in the grim words.

'Will you be all right?' They had reached the limousine. Horse Cromwell stepped in front of them and opened the rear door. He watched Karen discreetly, but intently.

'I'll be fine,' she said. 'You going off separately?'

'Business to see to,' Bennie Scroop said. 'I'll see you in a few days.'

They kissed quickly, then hugged.

'Anything you want,' Scroop said. 'Just ask.'

'I know.'

'For yourself or the boy . . .'

'Thanks, Dad.'

'And the Horse will be with you. Always on call.'

Karen turned and smiled at Horse Cromwell, who gave a quick smile back and nodded. Karen said, 'I'm glad about that.'

'Horse has always been with the family. And his father before him. I trust him like blood, Karen. Don't be shy of asking him for help.'

'I won't. Don't worry.'

Horse said, 'You make sure of it, now. Nothing's more important . . .'

Karen leaned towards him and kissed him. It looked as if she would kiss him on the cheek, but she hesitated and moved slightly so that her lips touched his. She held the kiss, then drew back, staring at Horse with a look that could only be described as pure interest.

Horse Cromwell blushed. He didn't meet Bennie Scroop's gaze, but tentatively took Karen's arm to assist her into the limousine.

On the slight hill to the south of the cemetery, George Bulman lowered a small pair of binoculars and rubbed his eyes. Standing next to him, Lucy McGinty let her irritation be known to her boss by the loudness and style of her breathing.

'I can handle this, George. I really can.'

'Just sizing up the opposition, Lucinda,' Bulman said, unfazed by his assistant's barely restrained wrath. 'Might come in useful should you . . . er . . . need advice, say?'

'You don't trust me is what you mean,' Lucy said.

'Teamwork is the name of the game,' Bulman retorted. Below them, the funeral party was rapidly dispersing among the long line of gleaming black cars.

'I'm a big girl now. I can look after myself.'

'Nothing Black and Decker down there can't fix.'

Lucy stared in grim silence at the group of men below. Now that the Scroop car had disappeared, voices and laughter drifted on the still, cold air.

'Bunch of thugs. But we'll sort them out, eh Georgie?'

With a thin smile Bulman murmured, 'Last bloke who said that's propping up Hammersmith Flyover.' He raised his glasses again, and scanned the grey faces below him.

Beside him, Lucy raised her Pentax camera and, through the telephoto lens, continued to snap the scene by the grave.

She took two frames more and reached the end of the film. But there was one image she was keen to see printed and blown up. The image of Karen Scroop kissing one of the heavies who had accompanied her father to the funeral.

Even from this distance it had been apparent that there was something not quite right about that moment's affection . . .

Chapter Five

He didn't dismiss Lucy's objections as being unimportant. He didn't ignore her words, nor the heartfelt emotion that had powered them. She was angry with him, and that meant a lot to George Bulman.

He was pleased she was angry. He had expected it. Nothing in the world would have stopped him following her to the funeral and checking out the mourners, for this face, or that, sussing out exactly what sort of opposition his young assistant would encounter on the street . . .

But he respected her the more for her resentment. She wanted responsibility, and she wanted it fast.

Too fast, of course, and if George Bulman was prepared to *think* about how relatively inexperienced his side-kick was, compared to himself, he was certainly not prepared to speak such patronizing words aloud.

Lucy was learning, and learning fast. He had never had such a good working relationship with anyone before. Despite her glum statement, he trusted her very much indeed. She was tenacious, no doubt an attribute of either her Irish or Scottish background, but the Celtic part of her, anyway. She was gritty, she was tough, she was determined . . .

She just wasn't very experienced yet, and she didn't have George Bulman's 'records library mind', his mental list of names and faces from all the years of his legitimate sleuthing for the Met.

'The Scroop family's a very nasty and solid old family,' he had said to her. 'They was slitting throats and cutting purses in the reign of Good Queen Bess . . .'

His memory didn't go back *quite* that far, of course.

Lucy McGinty had been unimpressed. 'I'll have you

know that the McGintys were outlaws in Connemara for more than two hundred years. *Wild* people they were—'

'With Scottish accents?'

'You'd have been lucky to hear the sound of their voices. They were quick and deadly. If they weren't outlaws they were pirates. When they settled in Scotland they lived in the ruins of crofts which they built up with their bare hands. During the winter of 1879 they competed with the jackdaws for the flesh of dead animals. The McGintys are a tough breed, George Bulman, and I'm proud to be one.'

'I'm sure you are, Lucinda. Just remind me not to visit your ancestral home too often.'

He felt more relaxed, now: about her being on the street, shadowing Karen Scroop.

And it gave him time, and the excuse, to get back to tracing the elusive Elias T. Greenstein.

Because, after all, there was a twenty thousand pound fee to come his way if he recovered Greenstein *lucrato intacta*.

His best bet, he decided, was Park Lane Autos. If they were straight they might well have had a record – or even a memory – of the man called Lawrence Culpepper . . . and therefore, possibly, of Elias Greenstein. In any event, the salesroom was worth a visit.

Despite its name, Park Lane Autos was nowhere near Park Lane. It was a wide-fronted building, all glass and shining radiators, with garish advertising pasted onto the inside. The cars – mostly Mercedes and Porsches – looked bright and new, but were noticeably (to the trained eye) second hand. The showroom was flanked by a seedy-looking Indian restaurant, and a bookmakers.

Dressed in his appallingly bright sports jacket, and his old school tie, Bulman walked inside. One hand in the pocket of his trousers, he strolled through the cars, checking for the red Bentley, but also checking out the small, weasel-faced man who sat behind the order-desk.

He was in his forties, well groomed, well dressed. When he saw that Bulman was staring at him he forced a smile and stood up, walking briskly over to the front plate-window where Bulman waited.

'Can I help you at all?'

Bulman smiled, hesitated as he kept the man's gaze. Then he said, 'What you got around thirty grand?'

Evidently George Bulman did not look like the sort of man who normally came in and spent big money. The salesman repressed a smirk and shook his head. 'Are you serious?'

Bulman let all the warmth and ease drop from his face. Steely eyed and hard, he stepped up close to the salesman and looked down at him.

'I was recommended by my friend . . .'

The salesman had gone white. He desperately tried not to meet Bulman's gaze, but the effect was hypnotic and he kept returning his stare to those narrowed, penetrating eyes.

'Your friend . . .?'

'Lawrence Culpepper.'

The salesman frowned. He backed off a little from Bulman, less frightened suddenly. 'You know Mister Culpepper?'

With a smile Bulman said, 'Intimately.'

'How is he these days?'

'Last time I saw him,' Bulman said easily, 'he was in the pink.'

'How strange . . .'

Frowning, Bulman asked, 'Why should that be strange?'

The salesman straightened his tie which was already perfectly straight. He strained to grow an inch, to stare Bulman straight in the eye. 'Because *I* am Lawrence Culpepper,' he said, and though his voice shook a little, he had invested the tone with a certain authority, now.

But George Bulman had been in this situation too many times to be either put out, or put off his stride. 'Is that right,' he said with a thin smile.

'Yes, it is,' Culpepper said. 'And you don't know me.'

'No sir. But I *do* know a gentleman called Elias Greenstein.'

The glimmering light of confusion shone briefly in Culpepper's eyes. 'Greenstein?'

'Greenstein.' Bulman leaned closer. 'And what I have to deduce is whether or not Greenstein is simply a *customer* of yours, or whether he's an accomplice . . .'

Confusion changed to alarm. 'Accomplice?'

With a quick movement, and a finishing flourish, Bulman presented his ID. Culpepper stared at the small card and picture. 'I'm an investigator, Mister Culpepper. In this case I've been retained by the Union Atlantic Bank. Obviously, when matters of a criminal complexion come to light I pass on my findings to the relevant police department.'

More alarm, this time tempered with growing confusion, with a touch of genuine bewilderment. 'Police?'

Bulman straightened up. 'Well, sir,' he said, not letting his gaze break from the salesman's. 'Embezzlement is still a crime on *both* sides of the Atlantic, as far as I am aware.'

'Embezzlement . . .' Culpepper breathed. He shook his head, his look almost pleading with Bulman. 'I lent him a car.'

'You *lent* him a car?'

Culpepper nodded quickly. 'I met him at an auction. Peter, that's the chap I share a house with . . . well, we're both rather keen on antique silver. Precious stones . . .'

Bulman stared hard at the thin-faced man, and himself felt a touch of confusion. He had had Culpepper down as an ordinary east-end sharpster, probably keeping a dolly-bird wife and a glam-child half his age. A gay antiques collector was one image Culpepper did *not* fit . . .

He shook his mind back to the question at hand. 'You were at an auction . . . Was Greenstein into the action?'

'Oh yes. He was a very pleasant chap. We all had a drink together and the next week he bought us a meal. At the Ritz.'

'That sounds like Elias T.,' Bulman muttered.

'He was quite charming,' Culpepper went on. 'When he told us that he had to take his widowed aunt down to the country – apparently she's loaded! – I lent him the burgundy Bentley.'

'And you got it back?'

'Certainly. He's now thinking of buying our Corniche. The blue one. Quite a bargain . . .'

'So you're in touch with him. Where is he now?'

'Well . . .' Culpepper thought for a moment. 'Since it's Wednesday, I'm sure he'll be at Wilkins and Mozarts.'

'Who're they when they're at home? Or shouldn't I ask . . .'

Culpepper looked vaguely offended. 'They're antique dealers. I'll give you the address.'

The auction rooms of Wilkins and Mozart, up west in Notting Hill, were small and tastefully furnished. Entering them was rather like entering the drawing room of a large stately home. Fifteen buyers sat in three rows of mahogany veneer chairs, facing a small podium where the auctioneer stood. Beside him, two young men in green overalls alternately presented the items for auction.

Bulman gained access to the room easily enough, and stood at the back for a few minutes, staring at the punters, deciding that he was absolutely sure he knew which was Greenstein, though it had been too dark at their last encounter to see the trickster's features clearly.

Elias T. was sitting in the middle row. He was not currently engaged in the bidding, but was favouring each person who – with the slightest wink or movement – was trying to acquire the silver candlesticks under offer with a long, hard look.

The whole place had an uncomfortable, hushed feel about it. Chairs creaked, catalogues rustled, and the auctioneer's voice was a gentle monotone.

'. . . Note the economy of design on this fine pair of silver chamber candlesticks, complete with snuffers and trimmers. Will anyone start the bidding at two thousand guineas? Thank you madam . . .'

Bulman glanced round in surprise. All he had heard or seen was a middle-aged woman coughing. He hoped she'd meant to make a bid.

'Do I hear two thousand five? Thank you, sir . . .'

Bulman stared in confusion. The man had simply wiped his nose with his fingers. He probably didn't even realize that he'd just bid twenty-five centuries for a couple of candlesticks that would have looked out of place in a junk shop.

No time to waste, however. Greenstein didn't seem to be involved in this bidding session either, so Bulman quietly edged forward and slipped into the seat behind the con-man.

Greenstein remained unsuspecting.

'Do I hear three thousand and fifty?' the auctioneer asked quietly. Bulman watched him, not really seeing him, as he leaned forward towards Greenstein's left ear.

'Thank you sir. Three thousand and fifty in the middle row. Do I hear seventy-five?'

Slowly it dawned on Bulman that he was the only man sitting in the middle row. He froze totally, his eyes wide, his mouth half opened, ready to whisper to Greenstein . . .

He didn't dare look round, even, to see if anyone else was still interested in bidding.

'Three thousand and fifty. Do I hear any advance?'

Yes . . . yes . . . wait for it. Give 'em a moment . . .

He wondered if the heat in his face, and the sudden cool sweat on his brow, was detectable by the American.

His agony ended. Somewhere in the room a wink, or a twitch, or a simulated heart attack signalled to the auctioneer that an extra twenty five pounds *would* be paid.

Merciful Lord. Keep thy light shining . . .

When the auctioneer looked at him he shook his head violently.

That was one message that *did* get through.

Now again he leaned close to Greenstein. The man nearly jumped out of his skin as Bulman's whispered voice told him that, 'Lawrence Culpepper sends his regards . . .'

How could so small and insignificant-looking a man be such a successful con-artist? Bulman found himself perplexed by the question as he walked with Greenstein out of the auction rooms. Although they walked with dignified ease, Bulman had his hand resting on the American's arm, and once out of eyeshot of the auctioneer, his grip became like a vice.

A small, weaselly looking man, better suited to a small desk in a ledger room somewhere . . . how appearance could give the lie to deeper talent!

Once in the street, Greenstein jerked his arm away, only to find Bulman holding on to him like a limpet.

'Let go of me, damn you!'

Bulman just smiled, his eyes narrowed and glittering with triumph. 'Never again, sunshine. The chase has been too long and you're one fish who's too slippery. Now. Where shall we chat?'

Greenstein glared at the larger man. 'Right here, buddy.'

'Suit yourself. You have taken the Union Atlantic Banking Corporation of New York City for two and a half million dollars.'

Greenstein just sneered, still tugging at his arm

which Bulman refused to release. 'What, l'il ol' me? Surely not.'

'Unless you come up with a serious settlement deal, Mister Greenstein, I will now take you to a police station where you will be arrested and held in custody pending extradition proceedings.'

Elias Greenstein took the statement into his head, staring all the time at the hard-faced P.I. The traffic roared along the main street next to them, almost drowning out the American's quietly asked question.

'You mean they don't have a contract out on me?'

'Contract?'

Frowning, as if he thought Bulman must have been stupid, Greenstein said loudly, 'A contract! You know . . . Bang Bang, you're dead. Or switch on auto-engine – Boom! Or automatic toothbrush, poisoned toothpaste . . .' He made a strangled sound. 'Or the elevator shaft, without elevator. *Splat!*'

It had never occurred to George Bulman that a bank would have taken out a contract on a man's life. He felt himself to be mildly shocked that Greenstein could even have imagined such a thing.

'Nobody's going to kill you,' he said.

'You're kidding, of course.' Deadpan. Unbelieving.

'Let me put it another way. *I'm* not going to kill you. I'm a legally registered private investigator, Mister Greenstein. My firm, S.T.G. – which stands for Sic Transit Gloria – are not going to kill *anyone*.'

Suspicious to the end, Greenstein looked at Bulman afresh, his face suddenly cannier, less hunted. 'So whadya want?' he murmured, the growl in his voice making him sound like the cheapest of New York hoodlums.

'Quite simple: my contract is either to take you in, for proper criminal proceedings, or to arrange for you to make a settlement.'

'A settlement? What sort of a settlement?'

'A monetary settlement. How much of the two and a half can you repay?'

With a gentle smile, glancing as a motorbike roared noisily past, Greenstein said, 'As of today?'

'Good place to start.'

'Eighteen hundred and sixty-three dollars. And forty-two cents.' He patted his trousers pocket. Loose change jingled.

Bulman was appalled. 'I don't believe you, Greenstein. I don't believe you for one tiny moment . . .'

'Too bad. It's the truth.'

'Where's the rest . . . ?'

'Let go my arm . . .'

'Where's the rest?'

'It's kinda tied up right now,' Greenstein said quickly as pain coursed through his muscles where Bulman's grip tightened as a vice tightens on wood. Bulman was getting very impatient with this cocky short-order from New York. 'I got this crippled aunt. Back in the States. No National Health, and she's dying. Of polio. I sent the money there . . .'

'Polio's a child's disease.'

'Not necessarily. It can strike at any time if you're not immune . . .'

'So can I, Sonny. So can I.'

Never letting his grip on the con-man relax for an instant, Bulman waved down a taxi, and the two of them took the long drive to the Isle of Dogs, where Dennis Holmes was stationed. Holmes was not at all happy to have his ordinary routine interrupted by a case on which he had *not* been working, but because of his 'other' involvement with Bulman, he could hardly refuse the request.

So Elias T. Greenstein was formally arrested, and dragged away—

'You got a heart of stone, fellah. My crippled aunt don't hear from me she's likely to relapse . . . Damn your black guts!'

—to an interview room, where a young P.C. would

spend an hour or two trying to make sense of any agreed statement that the American would volunteer.

Holmes fetched two black coffees from the vending machine, and joined George Bulman in the tiny office that served as his haven from the clatter of typewriters and bustle of activity in the main room of his department. Holmes' desk was covered with papers and half finished reports.

The man, just on the evidence of this clutter, was rattled and upset by things.

'Hell's teeth, George,' he said, as he sat behind his desk and sipped the disgusting instant brew. 'This is a right naughty one to land on a copper on a Wednesday afternoon.'

Propped on the edge of the desk, his jacket open, and his face beaming with inner contentment as he thought of a good job well done, Bulman just smiled. 'I thought you'd be glad of the collar, Dennis. Can't do you any harm. Two and a half million rip-off. And you the arresting officer. Beats blaggings and knife fights.'

Holmes scowled. 'I *like* blaggings and knife fights. Usually.' He glanced through the glass window at the tiny interview room, where Greenstein – staring at the mirror – knew he was being watched. 'Anyway. He hardly looks the type. You sure you got the right man?'

'Dead sure. That's how he did it, right? Appearance and the lie, Dennis. It's frightening how much we are affected by the look of people. That man has a lot upstairs. Believe me.'

'I believe you,' Holmes grunted. 'I'd still rather not handle it. What about Derek Willis? Your old oppo from the Yard.'

Bulman shook his head. 'He's on a job. Besides, they don't like bodies at the factory. Come on Dennis . . . do the decent . . .'

With a shrug, Holmes finally agreed. 'Okay, George. It's done. I can hold chummy for twenty-four hours, right? So you get working fast: his embassy, and the New York law. Fast, George.'

'I'm on my way. Just don't let him go.'

He placed his unfinished coffee on the table, and quickly gave it the last rites. Holmes led him to the door. 'How's my own little bit of business coming on?'

'Lucy's on it. Right now. Good lass that. Should have some results for you very soon. Now that Greenstein's safely off my hands . . .' he added pointedly.

Chapter Six

There was no question in Lucy's mind but that the tough-looking man whom Karen Scroop had kissed at the funeral was the man she would select for her vengeance mission.

Lucy developed and printed the whole reel of film which she'd taken at the cemetery, and enlarged half a dozen of the shots. Everything looked very normal, very ordinary . . . everything except the look between Karen and that man, in the instant after their cheeks had touched.

Lucy, feeling like David Hemmings in *Blow Up*, enlarged the shot to double-plate size, and stared at the blurred features, the grey smudges that were now details. Karen's face was half-turned to the camera, and there was an unmistakable smile on her lips. The man, so hard of face in other shots, looked open and loving, his eyes wide with concern, his lips parted in a uncertain smile, returned to someone for whom he had great – even adoring – respect.

'Got you my love . . .' Lucy whispered. 'Now to get *to* you . . .'

She placed the photograph on George's desk, then dressed warmly in a short jacket and jeans. She combed quickly through her hair, but removed all traces of make-up from her face, the better to melt into obscurity. Then she drove to the area where Karen lived, and began to stake out the house.

By early afternoon she was rewarded for her patience. Karen left the house, carrying a small basket, and climbed into the beige Camarro Coupé that was parked outside. She was dressed for seduction, a loose, semi-translucent skirt, sheer stockings, and a waistcoat over a white blouse. She looked tall, slim, full-figured, and her hair was immaculate.

The grieving widow . . .

The black widow spider . . .

And Lucy knew who the fly would be.

She followed at a discreet distance. Karen Scroop drove carefully, probably because the car was a new gift from her father and she was unused to the controls as yet. She stopped near the entrance to a small park, locked the car, and walked with the basket into the green space, strolling quickly along the pavement round the edge, towards a bench where a man sat.

The man Bulman had called 'Horse' Cromwell.

Lucy walked round the park the other way, getting as close to the couple as possible. To her annoyance she could not get into earshot, but she positioned herself so that she could *see* what was happening.

Horse glanced at her, and then stared for a few seconds, but Lucy just took out her sandwiches and a book, and began to read. After a while the intense scrutiny ended . . .

Just another drab little office worker out for a late lunch, she could hear Horse thinking.

Drab? Oh well . . .

But an office worker in jeans . . .

Lucy flushed as she realized that in her attempt to keep warm and look ordinary she had probably made herself look suspicious. On the other hand, she might well have looked like an attractive, but rather unkempt student, out for a late lunch, and the peace of the park studying a book.

Shirley Conran's *Lace* . . .

Feeling awkward again, Lucy bent the cover back so that it couldn't be seen, and drew a pen from her bag with which she began to pretend to annotate the margins.

After a while she risked a glance towards the other couple, and noted with satisfaction that Karen Scroop was coming on to Horse Cromwell with everything she'd got: eyes, smiles, and legs turned towards him, skirt hitched above her knees; her left hand rested gently on the man's left arm.

Body contact too.

Anything at all, she had decided that morning. *I'll offer anything at all. What the hell does it matter? It's for Dodger's sake, anyway. He wouldn't object. And if he wouldn't, who am I to be fussy . . .?*

She knew that Horse Cromwell had had a passion for her for years. He was not a man she found attractive, nor one whom she felt great respect for. His closeness to her father had meant that he'd been a regular visitor to the house, and a familiar figure in her world.

When Karen Scroop had reached the age of twelve she had first realized the deeper meaning behind Horse Cromwell's games with her, his looks, his playful squeezes and punches. He must have been a young man, then, twenty-five or so; and he had been behaving like a man of fifty, responding to the innocence and playful willingness of his boss's daughter.

At the age of eighteen, knowing the delights of freedom, exploring her senses and appetites with reckless abandon, she had thought very seriously about allowing Horse to be one of the two or three blokes a month she took on and tested for all-round suitability.

She was glad, now, that she'd resisted that impulse. The relationship would not have been the same . . . Horse would not have been so malleable.

For a tough man – a man who had at least three killings down to him – he was remarkably shy, and as she sat and chatted with him in the small park she could smell his sweat, and see how every deliberate pass she made at him sent a flush of colour round the part of his neck above his shirt collar.

It was like seducing monks in a monastery. Easy game.

'I want that copper topped, Horse. My Dodger was a good man, and the copper didn't have to have killed him. He'd been waiting his opportunity, and that's murder in my book . . .'

'Don't sound good,' Horse agreed.

'When my Dodger got blown away, a part of me was real hurt, Horse. His kid is hurt. And I'm hurt. You're my Uncle Horse, and you once told me that if anyone ever hurt me, you'd make sure they never hurt anything ever again. You remember saying that?'

Horse Cromwell nodded, not meeting her gaze. 'I remember.'

There was a moment of silence. Karen let her grip move slightly on his arm. She licked her lips, trying to look slightly sorrowful.

'Well . . .?'

'I dunno,' he said.

She leaned closer. Her hand slipped from his arm to his leg, a tentative touch that could have been communicating any one of several things, from unconscious emphasis to unsubtle desire. Horse responded to the touch by straightening slightly, and making his whole body go stiff.

'Horse . . .' Karen breathed. 'There's nothing in the world I want more . . .'

'I know, Karen. But . . .'

'And nobody else in the world that I'd ask. Just you, Uncle Horse. You're the only one who means enough to me to ask.'

Horse Cromwell was pleased. The flush spread farther round his neck. He gently patted the cool hand that rested on his thigh.

'Your Dad's the man to speak to,' he said.

Karen withdrew her touch, looked sad, looked depressed. 'He's more took up with running the Firm. He don't have time for affairs of honour.'

'I gotta do what he wants,' Horse said with a shrug.

'He never understood me,' Karen retorted glumly. 'Not like you did.'

'I'm sure he did, Karen . . .'

'No. We'd talk, we'd play. But I always felt distant.

But when you were around it was like being with a friend. That's why I'm glad you're here now, Uncle Horse.'

'Me too, Karen.'

'We had a special something. A special understanding.'

Horse smiled. Now it was *him* who reached out and patted her hand. 'You should have said all this to me before, Karen. You shouldn't have waited until you needed me so bad. I wouldn't have minded.'

'Wouldn't you? I wasn't sure. Since I got married I was afraid to express my feelings for you. I thought you'd be angry.'

'Not me, Karen.'

He realized she was staring at him. She watched him; she almost wanted to laugh as she saw the machinery churning away inside his head. That he was aroused was all too evident. That amused her too . . .

Anything at all. Who the hell cares?

He dangled on her line, a lifeless fish, resigned to being consumed. He didn't even struggle. All he could do was gaze into the distance, glance at her, see the look of love and desire in her eyes, and mutter *I dunno, I dunno.*

Uncertainty was a potent weapon. But he would run out of ammunition soon. It just took patience. It took acting. Karen thought of Dennis Holmes. She imagined the cut in his throat, gaping like a second mouth. Blood, death . . . and love. She became aroused herself. She shuffled closer to Horse.

'If you did what I want,' she whispered. 'Nobody would ever know.'

He looked at her. His face was pale, now, and there was sweat on it. The lost, uncertain look had gone. There was desire in his eyes, and decision . . . he was deciding to help her. He was believing that she felt lust for him, and not for an instant did he doubt that her lust was being fired by the lust for blood in the woman . . . but who cared? He had wanted Karen for years. Any way, any time.

She said, '*Anything* we do together, Uncle Horse. Nobody will ever know . . .'

Her hand brushed across his lap. It sent a shock through him that nearly made him gasp. She *touched* him. Her fingers hesitated, sensing him.

Touched him . . .

He shifted quickly, breaking the contact, straightening his tie. The student on the nearby bench kept on reading, not noticing the little scene being played out below the big lime tree.

'It wouldn't be right,' he murmured.

'Nobody,' Karen whispered, 'nobody would *ever* know. My Dodger may be dead, but there are things, even now, that a woman needs. I trust you, Horse. You must trust me. Help me . . . help me with that copper, and help me with . . . the other thing. Nobody will know. Our secret. It would form a bond between us that could never be broken.'

Horse turned to look at her. He looked at her mouth. He reached to kiss her, but Karen raised a hand, gently brushing his lips. She looked at the other people in the park.

'Not here . . .' she said.

They stood and walked back to their cars.

By early evening, in the detectives' room of the Isle of Dogs police station, the name 'George Bulman' had begun to sound like an obscenity. All afternoon, Dennis Holmes had been wading through the fine print and tangled complexities of the extradition laws between Britain and the United States of America. Greenstein was threatening very heavy action, and Holmes could find nothing that would allow him to hold the man beyond twenty-four hours.

He was beginning to sweat about it. It had taken his mind off the *other* thing, though. But it was still an infuriating drain on his time, and his energy, and his patience.

The phone jangled on a desk nearby, and Benson picked it up. All eyes in the room turned since this particular phone was the one used by the various snouts employed by the department.

'It's for you,' Benson said to Holmes. 'No code name.'

Holmes placed the sheaf of papers, and the book he'd been carrying, down on the desk and snatched the receiver from his colleague.

'Yeah . . . Holmes here.'

'Hello Mister Holmes. It's the bloke from the betting shop . . .'

'Right. What've you got for me?'

The snout was called Eddie. He was new on Holmes' book, but had twice come up quite usefully in the last two months.

'There's a meet arranged for eight thirty. Back of the old foundry. Buller's Wharf.'

'What sort of meet?'

Eddie dropped his voice a bit. 'A blagging. It's a Hatton Garden job. Big one. Look, meet me by the old watchkeeper's hut, okay? Eight o'clock. And bring some folding money.'

Holmes glanced at the paperwork to do with Greenstein. He was torn for a moment, torn between the need for duty, and the need to get out in the fresh air.

Fresh air won.

'All right. I'll be there. And thanks . . .'

Benson raised an eyebrow. 'Good tip?'

'Sounds like it. You know Buller's Wharf?'

'Yeah. Stake-out there once.'

'Where's the timekeeper's hut?'

Lucy continued to trail Karen Scroop for the rest of the day and into the evening. She was pleased with herself. Karen never suspected that she was being discreetly observed, and although Horse Cromwell had seemed, on an occasion or two in the park, to have been studying her a little too closely, he had never reacted as if he was suspicious.

The two of them went to a pub for an hour, then drove off separately. Whilst in the pub they talked to a small, scruffy-looking man, who remained behind.

When they parted company, Lucy was torn as to who she should follow. She followed Karen, saw the woman safely home, then – feeling mildly triumphant – returned to the clock shop in Shanghai Road.

Bulman was hard at work on a clock, face looking benign and content behind his gold half-frames. His Will Power T-shirt was stained with oily smudges.

'Good evening Lucinda. Happy hunting?'

She flung her jacket over a chair and stood by him, smiling down.

'Tea's made,' he said. 'You look like you could use some.'

'Karen's found her hit man,' she said proudly. 'I followed them for hours.'

'How *is* Horse these days?'

She was taken aback, momentarily stunned. How could he have known? He had spoilt the moment of her revelation.

'George! I've slaved for that. Creeping around blooming bushes, huddling in doorways . . .'

He looked up again and smiled. 'You only left a bleedin' great blow-up of the man on my desk . . .'

She remembered that, now, and looked crestfallen. 'Oh yes. So I did.'

'Anyway. It stands to reason . . .' He delicately adjusted a cog in the tiny timepiece that he was holding. 'Horse has always fancied Bennie Scroop's daughter. Do anything for her . . .'

Lucy slapped her hands together, thinking hard. 'Now we need evidence. How're we going to get that, I wonder?'

With a sardonic chuckle, Bulman said, 'The only evidence we're going to get is when Dennis Holmes steps into his motor one day and turns on the ignition. Boom bloody boom.'

'Why are you being so horrible?' she asked, shocked by Bulman's callousness.

'I told you. It's not a case we should've taken on.'

'Serious?'

'Serious.'

She watched him working for a moment, her face glum. 'But if you had a word with Horse. If you told him that if anything happened to Holmes he's number One in the frame . . .'

Shaking his head, Bulman said, 'He wouldn't care. Nobody'll prove it. And Karen *wants* the world to know she revenged her bloke.'

'There must be something we can do.'

'Sure. We can warn Dennis. Maybe he can fix Horse up with a cock and hen . . . it'll ease the pressure.'

'Cynical old bugger . . .' Lucy mumbled.

'Quite so. Now ask me where E. T. Greenstein is.'

He beamed up at her. She frowned, then realized what he meant. 'You've found him! You smart old gumshoe you.'

'Not so much of the old, if you don't mind. Yes. Greenstein is behind closed doors. In fact, Dennis is the arresting officer himself. Now you can give him a bell, congratulate him and warn him, both in one simple phone call. And our job is done. And it's down to the chipper for a slap-up meal.'

'I need more than fish and chips after what I've been through today,' Lucy grumbled, as she picked up the receiver and dialled Holmes' number.

Bulman stopped work and went upstairs to change. When he came down again, straightening his tie, Lucy was just hanging up the phone.

'Get through to him?'

'I left a message to ring back.'

'Where is he?'

'Out on a snout's meet. Something big going down.'

'All go for Dennis,' Bulman said, feeling slightly

irritated that the man wasn't sitting shotgun on Greenstein. 'Come on. Let's get our noses into the trough.'

Lucy shook her head. 'Go without me, George. Do you mind? I want to bath, freshen up.'

She wasn't happy. Bulman saw this, frowned, and came over to her. 'What is it, love? Not like you to turn your nose up at food.'

She shrugged. 'I'm anxious. About Dennis.'

'He's a big boy. By the time Horse gets around to tackling him he'll be well warned. Come and eat. I'm buying.'

She smiled. 'I'll see you in the Green Man. About an hour. How about that?'

'That's more like it. But for Gawd's sake put some paint on those pale, thin cheeks.'

'On your bike, George.'

Oh what joy, to breathe the air as a free man.

He strolled jauntily along the Shanghai Road. He saw a few folk he knew, and chatted with one or two he knew well. He even picked up a small alarm clock, from a fussy old biddy who came scurrying after him.

'You ain't hardly been open,' she complained. 'I been calling round all day. It's this clock. It just stopped. It needs help. Bad.'

'Thank you, madam. I'll do what I can. Shouldn't be no trouble at all.'

'You ought to be open,' she wheedled, her face a mask of crotchety complaint. 'It was an emergency. Call yourself a clock hospital.'

'We're not the bleedin' National Health,' he said, equally crustily. 'Call by in two days.'

He walked on, still very happy.

Greenstein's in the slammer. Slammer's got old Greenstein. Farewell old Elias. Go and do your rock time.

He whistled and hummed. He thought of the money he'd earned from the American bank, even though he'd not recovered the two and a half million.

Fish and chips tasted good. He stood eating them in the street, feeling relief at being off the Greenstein case pour through him like a cleansing stream.

When he'd eaten, he walked on to the Green Man. He ordered a double whisky at the bar, and chatted to his old friend, Ronnie Peters.

And it was as he drained the dregs of the first, and was turning to order a refill, that his knee began to tingle . . .

Ronnie watched him apprehensively.

'You all right, Georgie?'

'Yeah . . . no . . . I don't know . . .'

The knee nagged. The tingle became a pain. He rubbed it, frowning as he tried to think what it could be.

'Rheumatism, George?'

Bulman looked up at his mate. He straightened up, stared into the middle distance . . .

'Not rheumatism. A blinding flash of light, Ronnie! I'll be seeing you . . .'

And he ran from the bar, turning left onto the main road and scampering towards the phone box he could see.

Lucy had finished her bath when the phone rang. Draped in a towel, chewing on a jam sandwich, she plucked the receiver from its cradle. Through a full mouth she said, 'Hello?'

'You said a snout's meet!'

The voice was familiar. A breathless, male voice, a voice filled with anxiety.

'George?'

'A meet!' Bulman shouted. 'You said a snout's meet. Dennis.'

Perturbed by his tone of voice she swallowed quickly, then sat on the edge of the desk. 'That's right. He won't be back.'

'That's what I'm afraid of,' Bulman said.

'What d'you mean, George?' she began, and then grasped *exactly* what he meant. 'Oh my God. A trap.'

'Lucy. Bell the Isle of Dogs nick. Speak to Jim Benson. That's Dennis's partner. Get him round to the Dauphin Sporting Club soonest.'

Lucy understood. 'That's Bennie Scroop's place, right?'

'Correct. And when you get there, keep Benson in the car outside. Or the game's a bummer.'

'And Dennis?'

Bulman hesitated just a second. Then he said, 'Depends what they've set up for him. If we blow this, I don't rate his chances. Not one little bit.'

Chapter Seven

As he approached the dock area around Buller's Wharf, Dennis Holmes cut the headlights of his BMW and slowed to a quiet stop by the side of the road.

He sat for a few minutes staring into the gloom, watching for movement. The whole area was a waste-land of derelict buildings, cracked concrete roadways and deserted warehouses. Their walls rose, grey and featureless, into the night sky. A few lights, mostly across the river, cast thin shadows on the roadways and against the sides of buildings that had long since ceased to bustle with trade.

At length, Holmes stepped from the car, quietly closed the door, and walked steadily towards the water's edge. The water of the dock glimmered with the street lights of Woolwich. It lapped gently against the wharf, a sound that always made Holmes edgy. It could have been the sound of someone slowly swimming towards him, and he unconsciously looked for movement among the restless reflections of the lamps.

Hands in his pockets he walked towards the low building that was the old foundry. Its high doors were closed, all its windows smashed. Beside it, the time-keeper's hut was a simple lean-to, its door ripped from the hinges, its windows dark.

A small man stood there, hunched inside an overcoat. He looked nervous. He was smoking a cigarette and the tip glowed in the semi-darkness.

Holmes walked up to him. Eddie dropped the cigarette and ground it out with his shoe. He smelled unpleasant, unwashed. When he looked up at Holmes there was something animal in his eyes, that mad look that tells of the fight for survival which occupies most of a creature's living day.

'Hello Mister Holmes. Nice to see you . . .'

'Hello Eddie. How's life?'

'Moves along. Can't complain.'

Holmes looked around. The whole place seemed deserted. Cars whined in the distance. Their lights flickered and vanished. It added to the eerie sense of desolation around this wharf area.

'Right then. Where's this meet?'

'I'll take you there,' Eddie said, but he made no move.

'Who's involved?' Holmes asked.

'It's a firm you've been after a long time, Mister Holmes.'

'There's lots of those, Eddie. Be more specific.'

Eddie shuffled uncomfortably. He looked around. His eyes flickered and glinted as he tried to meet Holmes' gaze, but couldn't quite manage it.

'You know my code, Mister Holmes. Tell you what it's about, but never mention the Firm by name. But it's worth a couple of centuries, I swear.'

'Oh yeah?' Holmes had heard that before. He drew out a small wad of notes and peeled off three. 'Here's thirty nicker on account. Okay? If the Firm's a big one, then maybe we'll talk a century on top.'

Eddie hesitated, then snatched the money, nodding curtly. He'd clearly hoped for more 'on account' but he knew it wasn't worth arguing with Holmes. Holmes was always as good as his word.

'Why're you so nervous, Eddie?'

'Why d'you think? I get seen round here I get an extra mouth in the neck region. And I'm cold. I want to get this over with . . .'

'Let's go then.'

Eddie still seemed edgy about something, almost puzzled, Holmes thought. He kept looking back the way Holmes had come.

'Where's your team?' he asked eventually.

'Didn't bring it,' Holmes said, understanding, now: if he'd brought the team with him there would have been the possibility of a raid, and Eddie might have got caught in that, or at least seen. 'All I want tonight is a look at the faces. Be ready for them on the day.'

Eddie seemed satisfied by that. He led the way through the shadows, into the echoing space of a large warehouse. It smelled of dust and decay. There were recesses in the side walls, black pits in the gloom, and Holmes went to one and stepped out of sight. Eddie shuffled about for a minute, looking around, then said, 'This is where the meet'll be. About half an hour.'

'Ta, Eddie.'

'I'll push off, then.'

'You do that.'

Holmes watched him go. Whatever happened, whoever turned up, he'd keep Eddie down to seventy quid. No point in over-paying this early in the game. Eddie was going to be useful for a few months.

The minutes passed. It was cold, and Holmes' legs were aching. He realized he wanted to urinate, but that wasn't on. He also fancied a drink. A nice Scotch whisky. To warm himself up.

Then he thought he heard a sound, a stealthy movement. He glanced at his watch. Twenty minutes early. The sound didn't come again, and he put it down to the breeze.

He folded his arms, huddled deeper into his coat, and became a shadow among shadows.

Bulman arrived at the Dauphin Club before Lucy, but that wasn't surprising. Just so long as she was there when he came out! He crossed the road from the taxi and walked straight into the tastefully-lit interior. Gentle music wafted from the gaming room, as did the sound of wheels spinning and voices murmuring.

As Bulman made to walk into the main club area, beyond which was the door leading to Bennie Scroop's private office, a tuxedoed minder stepped in front of him.

The man was young, early twenties; his shoulders

were broad, his clothes well cut, his eyes hard, his face smooth. Strong as an ox, the last thing he really wanted – Bulman intuited – was trouble.

Bulman stopped and stared at him. The minder smiled thinly. 'Where the hell do you think you're going?'

Punk, Bulman thought, but externally he just smiled. 'Where's Horse Cromwell?'

'Who wants to know? You a friend of his?'

'More of a business acquaintance. Is he here?'

'Not at the moment, no.'

'Fine,' Bulman said evenly. He looked past the minder. 'I'll have a word with Bennie, then.'

'You mean Mister Scroop . . .' the minder said pointedly.

'Mister Scroop,' Bulman agreed patiently, and – still smiling – pushed past the younger man.

The younger man reached out a hand that could have crushed a football and eased Bulman back from the gaming-room door. Bulman turned face on to him and moved forward so that his face was just an inch from the minder's face.

He let the smile play about his lips, a hard, humourless smile. The minder's face registered uncertainty. The arrogance began to drain away.

'Sonny,' Bulman said. 'You're a good boy for your boss. But that won't help you regain the use of your legs. Be very wise and we'll forget all about it.'

And he gently pushed the young man aside and stepped into the gaming room.

He walked quickly through the punters to one of the two doors marked private. He walked straight in, surprising Bennie Scroop, who was lounging at his desk smoking a cigar. The minder hovered behind Bulman until Bulman closed the door on him. 'Hello, Bennie.'

'Bloody George Bulman. And my horoscope said nothing unpleasant would happen to me today.'

'Can't trust those things, Bennie.'

'Lots of things you can't trust these days.'

'Like partners, for instance,' Bulman prompted. Scroop stared at him.

'Who d'you mean, Georgie? Horse?'

'Where is he, Bennie? Where is he right now?'

'Looking after Karen,' Scroop said, but from his face Bulman knew that he was suddenly edgy.

'The hell he is, Bennie. He's about to top that copper. Karen's talked him into it, and he's doing it. For love.'

Bennie Scroop stubbed out his cigar. He looked worried, as much as he could ever register such an emotion. 'You sure?' he murmured.

'Dead sure, Bennie. And worried. Worried enough to come here and get your help.'

'Damn,' Scroop said vehemently. 'Damn, *damn*. I told her not to . . .' He looked up. He said nothing.

Bulman said, 'If Horse kills Dennis Holmes your whole enterprise is for the bulldozer. You know that, don't you Bennie?'

'It's all circumstantial,' Scroop said, clutching at straws.

George Bulman straightened up. 'Fine. You sit there and count tonight's takings. We'll play a little betting game, a little bluff. You'll bet that Karen *hasn't* persuaded Horse Cromwell to murder a Metropolitan D.I. And I'll take the bet . . .'

He waited. Scroop waited. The atmosphere grew tense, and Bulman began to think that Scroop would not, actually, believe his daughter capable of such an act.

He was wrong. Bennie Scroop suddenly rose to his feet, grabbed his jacket, and led the way out of the club.

As they stepped into the night, Bulman saw Lucy's tiny car, parked fifty yards away. There was someone else in the car with her, and he smiled. Good old Lucy, and her persuasive tongue. She'd got Benson to come out.

'Why don't you wait in your motor, Bennie,' Bulman said to Scroop. 'I'll try and find out where they are.'

Scroop followed his gaze to the Citroen, then scowled. 'Bulman, you've got to swear: no rozzers. Let me handle it alone.'

'We won't have any rozzers if I can avoid it,' Bulman muttered. 'But that depends on a lot of things, Bennie. A lot of things.'

As Bennie Scroop walked slowly to his own car, Bulman went over to the 2CV and leaned down to talk to Jim Benson. The policeman was frowning. He was watching Scroop, and he was watching Bulman, and he was trying to figure out what was going on.

'Where's Dennis Holmes?' Bulman asked bluntly. Benson stared at him, then narrowed his eyes. He tried to play it tough.

'I come down here with your bird because that's my job. Now *I* ask the questions, sport . . .'

As he spoke he opened the car door and began to get out. Bulman slammed him back into the seat, and closed the door again.

He said, 'Step out of this motor, *sport*, and you'll frighten off the best chance we have of seeing Dennis alive.'

Benson was furious. He wasn't used to being pushed around. *He* always did the pushing. It narked him when the tables were turned. Fuming, he breathed, 'This time, pal, you *are* nicked.'

'Belt up, Benson,' George Bulman snapped. He had no time for these histrionics. 'Your skipper has been lured to a meeting where I suspect an attempt may be made on his life.'

'I'm getting out of the car,' Benson said, and again tried to open the door. Again, Bulman slammed it shut.

'Benson. Unless you want a death on your conscience, start behaving like a detective and not like a noddy on points duty. Look. I got Bennie Scroop over there. He's waiting for the word to interrupt the meet and stop one of his minders who's got a bit naughty.'

Benson said nothing, just stared, white-faced and furious.

Lucy said, 'It's about the Dodger Tait killing.'

With an expression of deepest irritation, Benson almost snapped her head off. 'I *had* deduced that!'

'Well that's something, at least,' Bulman murmured deliberately. He crouched by the window. 'Come on, I know Dennis. He would leave a hint.'

After a moment's tense silence, Benson nodded his head. 'The timekeeper's hut. Old foundry back of Buller's Wharf.'

'Ace . . .'

Bulman straightened up, calculating quickly how long it would take to drive from here to that part of the dockland.

Benson said, 'I'll have to get onto it. You know that.'

'Just let me get off first with Scroop. He doesn't want this any more than we do.'

'Yeah, I'll bet.'

'And Benson . . .' Bulman stooped again, and fixed the young policeman with his most feral gaze. 'No cavalry, eh? I know the villain in question. Flashing blue lights make him very violent . . .'

He could almost *feel* the impatience building up in the waiting man. It was a good feeling. And he could smell him, too, the faint hint of nervous sweat, breath going stale . . .

Horse Cromwell smiled to himself as he stood in the darkness, just twenty feet from the silent policeman. It was well after time, and Holmes would even now be weighing the options: the meet had been called off; he'd been set up by the runt, Eddie; he'd been seen when he'd arrived and scared them away . . .

All the thoughts, all the possibilities . . .

There could only be one result: he'd walk slowly and quietly back towards his car, abandoning the stake-out, furious, but resigned to the fact that the evening had failed.

When he walked he would walk right past the alcove where Horse was waiting for him.

Horse gently touched the blade again, feeling its cool length, testing its edges, honed to razor sharpness. It was eight inches long, half an inch wide . . . if you turned it edge-on, it almost vanished.

It would slide in and out of the copper's body in less than a second. It would thrust deep, snicking through the arteries above the heart. It would go so fast, so cleanly, that Holmes probably wouldn't even know he'd been stabbed.

He might stay standing for twenty seconds before the pain came. And when the pain came, he'd be dead.

He hardly breathed. He closed his eyes and thought of Karen's body, how it had felt, so cool and soft and supple. He thought of the way she would welcome him when the job was done. He thought of a lot of things, things she'd promised . . .

Take your time, copper. Take your time. I'm happy with my dreams . . .

Damn you, Eddie. Damn you to hell, you poxy little runt . . .

Holmes looked at his watch, cupping his hand around the luminous dial.

They weren't coming. The meet would not happen. Either Eddie had set him up, or the *runt* had been set up. In either case, there was no point in standing here any more, freezing slowly to death.

It was always possible, he supposed, that the meeting had been changed *after* Eddie had eavesdropped on the conversation. But the time to find that out would be tomorrow.

Right now: time to go.

Holmes still walked quietly. It was – as a last likelihood – just possible that the meeting was happening right now, round a corner, or in another part of the derelict wharf. So Holmes stepped carefully as he began to make his way back to the open air, back to his car.

And as he walked so the hair on his neck pricked: he had the uncanny feeling he was being watched. He hesitated and looked around, but there was just darkness in various shades. He shrugged and walked on, towards the gaping open end of the warehouse.

And a car hummed past, and turned to face him.

For a second he was too shocked to react. He stood stock still, watching the sleek dark shape. A BMW. Headlights off. Two men inside.

Something about the car tickled his memory, and after a second it came to him. Bennie Scroop.

Well I'm damned . . .

So it was a set-up after all. Scroop come to see about the killer of his daughter's husband. Quite why Holmes smiled at that moment he might have been hard put to say. Maybe he just felt that the elder Scroop wouldn't have dared risk his life, and his Firm, by being personally involved in killing a policeman.

Holmes felt – peculiarly enough – safe.

The car's headlights came on, fixing him in their glare. He squinted and turned his head away from the brilliance.

Horse Cromwell was standing four feet away, staring at him, face white with shock, a knife in his hand!

Nothing happened. The two men just stared at each other, each equally startled. Then a voice called, 'Horse! Clear off, the lilly's on its way!'

Horse Cromwell trembled. He took a half step forward, then took its back. He glanced at the car, at his boss, then fixed Holmes with that look again, the killer look, the look that said, 'I've got to do this . . .'

The knife gleamed in the headlights. Horse was just out of reach. He'd have to step forward first, but he would be quick, Holmes knew that. When he moved it would be like lightning.

'Horse!' Scroop shouted again. 'Leave it out. We know you only meant to frighten him!'

Horse shook his head. Still undecided, he must by now have felt himself too far committed. His thin face seemed calm, his eyes glittered like hard jewels.

Holmes said, 'Go on, Horse. Buzz off. We'll forget it. I understand . . .'

Horse Cromwell trembled again and frowned. He glanced at the car, then back at his victim, and slowly, very slowly, he took a step backwards.

Holmes' heart was racing. He consciously tried to stop the seepage of sweat from his face, but failed. But he tried to look calm, even though he was giving himself away.

And then: the siren. A police car screeched into view, blue light flashing.

It all happened so fast. One moment Horse had been giving up, the next he had panicked. He screamed something, and if what he screamed were words, they made no sense to Dennis Holmes. All Holmes knew was that Horse was running at him . . .

The knife was flashing up, a deadly curve towards his stomach . . .

There was a shot, a dull sound in the big space. Horse Cromwell seemed to twist and dance, arms flailing. The knife clattered off the concrete wall of the building. Horse's body crumpled on the ground, twitching and trembling, blood pooling below the head.

On the other side of the headlights George Bulman broke out of his stunned trance. He had just managed to swear at the sound of the siren when it had all – incredibly – been over.

Bennie Scroop lowered his arm. He looked down at the Smith and Wesson automatic, then glanced at Bulman and held the gun towards him. Bulman took the weapon and emptied it.

'Had to be done,' Scroop whispered. Strangely, Bulman felt like comforting him. He had not seen that Bennie was aiming a pistol at his colleague. All the time he'd been shouting at Horse, he'd had Horse in the sights of his gun.

No way was Bennie Scroop going to let a policeman die for the sake of Dodger Tait. He valued his daughter's liberty too much for that.

Holmes came up, visibly shaken. 'Thanks,' he said to Scroop. 'You saved my life. I appreciate that.'

Scroop just stared at him coldly.

Holmes went on, 'I'm going to have to charge you, Bennie. You know that.'

'Course I know that.'

'But the D.P.P.'ll see it as reasonable force. I doubt you'll even go down.'

Bennie Scroop stepped up to the policeman and stared him straight in the eye. Holmes looked deeply uncomfortable.

'You caused the death of an old and trusted friend,' Scroop whispered. He paused, then added, '*Now* it's personal . . .'

Jim Benson tugged at his sleeve and he turned away, not glancing at Bulman. He was led to a police car. Benson got in after him.

'So nearly an even result,' Bulman muttered.

'Dunno, George,' Holmes said. 'Horse was committed. If he'd got off this time he'd have had another go. I know that, now. It's something I'll live with.'

'You don't think it's finished then,' Bulman asked him, curious as to how the policeman's mind was working. A couple of days ago Holmes had been panicking. Now he seemed . . . cool.

'It'll be a while before it's finished, George. Young Karen's an evil little moll. She'll find another mug.'

'But you'll be ready for it, this time . . .'

Holmes smiled. 'Name of the game.'

Slapping his hands together, Bulman injected a more cheery note into his voice. 'Well at least you've got a multi-million-dollar fraudster under your belt. That can't be bad.'

Holmes looked awkward, smiling guiltily. 'I forgot to tell you, didn't I . . .'

'Tell me what?

'Just before I left the nick to come here . . . we found out that that wasn't Greenstein . . .'

'I don't want to hear this,' Bulman murmured weakly.

'Just some little con artist Greenstein'd been paying to keep the heat off. We had to let him go.'

Bulman closed his eyes, clenched his fists.

'Bloody Greenstein! Bloody ponce Greenstein! This means war!'

PART TWO

One of our Pigeons is missing

Chapter Eight

On the morning that the Professor's body was found, Jack Straw was up below the skylight of the converted warehouse, waiting impatiently for his special visitor.

He had been aware for some hours that there was a restless feeling about the group of tramps who inhabited the sheltered recesses of the derelict quayside. As he watched them from the loading bay, the group of men – and one woman, Rosy – seemed to be moving less busily than usual. There were conversations and agitated gestures. The drably dressed group were upset about something.

Jack Straw had other things on his mind than the pathetic worries of the group of hoboes. He lived uneasily close to them, separated in distance by a height of sixty feet. In many ways he felt – quite literally – above them. He spent his days watching the sluggish water of the canal, and the activity in the distance, towards Manchester, where the docklands were still used. The tramps seemed oblivious of anything but the crumbling walls, the fire-pits and the concrete quayside of their ruined kingdom.

Straw again raised his binoculars to his eyes, and scanned the grey-blue skies to the east for a sign of the bird. He spoke the bird's call name – Panama – murmuring it aloud several times as if his urgently whispered invocation would somehow affect the pigeon's flight plan.

Panama had never been *this* late before. Perhaps something had gone wrong.

Straw's castle was littered with pigeon cages, feathers, packets of food (for both bird and man) and the scattered straw which both species of occupant of this high, deserted place used for comfort. It had taken the man many weeks to create this haven out of the decaying remnants of the warehouse. He had installed a ladder from ground to loading bay – *inside* the building – and guarded access with aggressive fervour.

This was *his* place. His and no one else's. Except the pigeons, of course.

The hen pigeon that was waiting for Panama cooed and strutted inside her cage. Proud, pointed faced, bright-eyed: in her bird-like way she was a perfect mimic of the small, sharp-faced man who protected her.

Out on the water a ship's siren gave two long blasts. The sound of metal banging against metal drifted to the place of derelicts: another ship weighing anchor and slipping her river berth.

Straw turned to watch it, wondering for where it was headed, and what adventures it might have on the way. He was fifty years old and had been a seaman himself for thirty of them. He missed the sea. He quite missed the hard work.

It was the company of men he hadn't been able to cope with, a social claustrophobia that had driven him to his solitary existence in this cold, windy place above the ruined concrete strand.

He watched the tramps as they bustled and huddled. A fire burned in the lee of an old, part-demolished office building. Green Hat stood staring through its empty window at the canal. Rosy was snapping twigs to feed the fire, and looking concerned, he noticed. The others were huddled in various places, though the Professor wasn't with them. Not surprising. Straw wondered how many of the group below were party to what *he* knew . . .

Back to the sky, searching the wide blue with his high-powered lenses.

And after a few minutes he saw the tiny black speck that he knew would be his pigeon. Even the hen seemed to sense Panama's coming. She strutted more restlessly, ducked and glanced with glitter-eyed excitement.

The pigeon swept wide around the canal, circled once above the warehouse, then dropped for a landing that by anybody's standards was precisely pointed, but rather too fast. The bird skidded on the straw-littered sill of the skylight.

'Welcome, my beauty . . .' Straw said happily, and reached up for the bird, stroking it gently. He took Panama to the cage where the hen waited, and the two birds began to chatter frantically.

'Don't be impatient, little one. You can have your fill of her in just a moment . . .'

As he whispered softly so he slipped the binding of the small tube on the bird's leg. The tube was black, about an inch long. It came away, and Straw released the bird to its loved one.

He closed the cage door and walked to the wide mouth of the loading ramp, leaning against the wood and idly watching the tramps as he unfurled the small piece of paper and looked at its pattern of meaningless dots.

Below him there was a sudden buzz of conversation. The tramps were all standing, and walked slowly towards the canal. Straw frowned. He noticed that the retired priest, O'Dowd, was among them, a tall man in a dark, ill-fitting suit. He had come to recruit the hoboes for his soup and song session.

Something had interrupted his visit.

Straw couldn't see what was happening. The tramps were gathering by the wharf steps, out of sight behind a second warehouse. He climbed down his ladder and walked to the quayside, and used his binoculars to watch the group.

O'Dowd and Green Hat were on the steps, dragging at something in the water.

It took Straw only a moment to recognize that that something was a body, floating face down.

'And so, goodbye Professor,' he murmured quietly, before returning to his pigeon loft.

The police would come, he knew, and that would be a nuisance. They'd ask questions, they'd sniff around, but it would soon be over. He was confident that they'd take no notice of his pigeon place.

Straw felt quite happy about things. Until three days later, when a new arrival made himself known among the tramps . . .

He'd arrived during the night. Green Hat saw him first, walking along the canal side, a bulky silhouette against the half-full moon. He'd stopped and watched the fire, and the tramps gathered round it had turned to stare at the sinister shape.

Rosy had whimpered slightly. 'It's 'im. 'E's come back.'

Green Hat had soothed her. 'He's dead, Rosy. He ain't coming back.'

'It's 'is ghost.'

'Put on weight, then.'

The stranger came a little closer. The fire cast a faint yellow glow across him. He was wearing a long overcoat, tied at the waist with string. His head was warmly encased in a grey balaclava. He carried a strange-looking pack on his back, but when he turned away and went over to a nearby wall the group around the fire realized what it was.

Boxes. Cardboard boxes. The quiet man slowly put them together, straightening them out before folding them. In this way he made a sort of shelter, a box tent, and he wriggled inside and stayed there until morning.

Shortly after dawn he squirmed out of his box hut, stood and stretched. Rosy fussed with the fire. Spanish was collecting wood from the canal, to be dried out. Green Hat was stamping his feet briskly, trying to get his blood to circulate. Green Hat felt the cold a lot, and he was beginning to suffer quite badly. Rosy knew the signs, the first signs. She felt bad about it.

The stranger walked to the canal side. His breath frosted slightly in the crisp dawn air. He unloosened his overcoat and urinated, unselfconsciously, into the green water. Green Hat waited until the ablutions were finished, then walked over to him, curious. The new arrival was a well-built man, full in the face. He looked well fed. He smelled funny, too. Not like a man who'd been on the road for months. He smelled too sweet.

But he was also familiar. Green Hat had seen him before.

'You carry your house with you,' Green Hat said, coming up beside the other man.

'It's a *dop*,' the man said.

'Never 'eard of it.'

'South African. Temporary house. Been carrying it with me for a year.'

Green Hat looked at the boxes and nodded. It was a good idea. He looked back at the stranger.

'Seen you round 'ere before.' It was cold and he slapped his hands together. The stranger wore thick gloves with cut-away fingers. He looked warm.

'Meaning you 'aven't,' the stranger said.

And then Green Hat remembered. 'The Quiet Man, we called you. I *do* remember. The Quiet Man.'

'That fire's dying,' Quiet said, and shook his head at the same time. 'Not me . . .'

'A few years back. Liverpool.'

'Nah. Somebody else.'

Green Hat was sure of himself, though. On the bomb-site, close to the B&I Ferryport. The Quiet Man had spent two weeks or more with them, and then had vanished as mysteriously as he'd come . . .

'You was pally with the Professor,' Green Hat insisted.

'Who's that?'

'The Professor. That's 'is doxy over there.'

They both looked at Rosy. Swathed in coats, head buried beneath a big woollen hat, it was hard to tell whether it was male or female that sat there, desperately trying to rescue the fire. Her pram was next to her as always, and the small, scruffy mongrel was tied to the pram, and quietly waiting for a morsel to eat.

Quiet stared at her for a long time. Then he looked around and Green Hat looked with him. They both, in this way, saw the dark figure of Jack Straw standing in the loading bay above them, watching curiously.

Quiet turned back to the other. 'Don't remember you, though.'

'Green Hat they call me.' He rubbed his hands against the chill, and smiled through his whiskers. Quiet stood there, staring at his head, which was covered by a blue scarf. 'Shoulda known. Yeah . . .' Quiet looked away. 'The Professor. I remember him.' He paused for a moment. 'Tea bags. He always had tea bags.'

'Only one,' Green Hat said.

'Kept it in a parking ticket for safety.'

'Parking ticket holder,' Green Hat gently corrected.

Quiet glanced up at him. It was too penetrating a look, too consciously a glance of interest. It didn't fit with a tramp, and Green Hat felt uncomfortable. Quiet asked, 'Where is 'e?'

'Dead. Murdered . . .'

'Poor old Prof.' They stared at the lapping waters of the canal. 'Who did it?'

But Green Hat had had enough. It wasn't that he didn't like the stranger, he just felt uncomfortable with the questions.

'Fire's dying,' he said, and turned away.

Quiet called after him. 'What happened to your green hat?'

'I lost it.'

Quiet smiled to himself, then turned to half-look at the man in the warehouse who was still watching the scene below.

When he'd packed up his boxes, Quiet walked over to where Rosy was loading all her worldly possessions into the battered pram. This seemed to consist mostly of shoes and firewood. The unhappy-looking dog lay slumped by the wheels, almost mournfully watching the dying fire.

Quiet said, 'Moving on, eh?'

'Mind yer own business,' Rosy said. Her voice was hoarse, like the voice of someone who's smoked too much, or been crying.

Quiet shuffled about for a moment, watching her. Then he said, 'Bloke driving past down the old crane site throws out a half cigar. Big 'un. Don't use 'em meself.'

Rosy glanced up, and looked at the half half-corona that Quiet was holding. Then she shook her head. *Mind yer own* . . . But she was only half hearted, now.

'What you going to do wiv it?' she asked.

'Bit of a waste . . . on me. Trade it, I expect.' He reached down to pat the dog. 'Hello boy.'

Rosy watched him, straightening up slightly now that her packing was done. 'What would you take for it? Dearie . . .' she added as an afterthought.

'What you got?'

'What size feet?'

'Twelve.'

She rummaged around in the pram. 'I got a ten . . . in brown. Eight and a half. Nine . . . Ah, 'ere we are.' She pulled out a tattered running shoe. 'That's a twelve.' She rummaged for the partner, then held the boots towards Quiet. When he didn't immediately take them she rummaged again and placed two small firelighters on top.

Without a word Quiet took the boots and passed over the cigar. Rosy took it, stuck it in her mouth, and just tasted it. 'How'd you know I was partial to these?'

'Professor told me.'

She stared at him. Then she looked at the smoke, rolling it gently between her fingers. She seemed upset. ' 'E got done in.'

'I heard.' He struck a match from a matchbox and held it to the woman. After a moment Rosy bent her head and lit the cigar, puffing contentedly. 'Who done it?' Quiet asked.

'Dunno.' She inhaled too deeply and was racked by a coughing fit, which brought tears to her eyes. When her lungs were functioning again she sat down by the fire, and Quiet sat down with her.

'You were mates, weren't you? You and the Professor . . .'

Rosy nodded, gazing out across the dereliction that had been her world for nearly a year. Distantly, machinery began to thump and metal rattled. 'More'n four years, Quiet. That's a long time.'

'Who would want to kill 'im? I mean . . . where had he just been, Rosy? The days before the . . . before you found him?'

Rosy frowned, thinking hard. But all she said was, 'I wanted to go to Lincoln. That's where I'm going now. Lincoln . . .'

And then she went quiet, hardly moving except to lift the cigar to her lips. Quiet stood up and moved away, hands in his pockets. He walked along the quayside, out of sight of the sheltered place where the tramps had their home. He stood at the steps where the Professor's body had been found, then slowly walked down them and sat at the bottom, feet almost touching the cold water.

A shadow touched him. He heard movement behind him, and wasn't surprised, when he turned, to see the man from the warehouse, the Watcher, the man the tramps called Straw.

Up the canal a way a ship's siren hooted three times.

Straw glanced in its direction, then said, 'I am going astern.'

'You wot?'

'Three blasts. Ship code. I am going astern.'

Quiet stood up and walked back up the steps, appraising the small man carefully. 'Nautical sort of bloke, are you?'

'You're the Quiet Man, right?' Straw said, ignoring the question.

'What's in a name?'

'Saw you talking to Rosy.'

'Saw you watching us. Nosy bleeder, ain't you?'

'So you ain't so quiet,' Straw said, discomforted by the tramp's directness.

Quiet looked at him, 'You see the Professor that last day?'

Straw walked around him, and Quiet turned to keep his gaze on the smaller man. Straw smelled of pigeons. He had nervous mannerisms, little glances, fluttering movements of his hands – bird-like.

He said, 'They say his throat was cut. Ear to ear. Very nasty.'

'Earlier. Did you see him earlier . . . *before* 'e got topped?'

'You ask a lot of questions. Hardly call you quiet . . .'

'Yeah. But I was an old friend of the Professor's. Don't seem right.'

Quiet looked at the water, then smiled. 'Where could we get a boat?'

'What for?'

'Go for a sail.'

'No chance.' Straw relaxed a little. 'I was on a boat once. Stoker by trade. We went some places that were real hot and sunny. People were brown like . . . like a brown snooker ball . . .' As he spoke he fingered the neck of a sherry bottle, protruding from his jacket pocket. Quiet was watching the bottle and looking agitated.

'What ship was that?'

'Questions,' Straw said with an evil grin. 'Always questions. Torquemada I think we'll call you.'

Still eyeing the sherry bottle, Quiet said, 'Big words for a dosser.'

'Not a dosser. Got my own house. Got pigeons too.'

'Give you a firelighter for a swig.'

Straw laughed sneeringly, did the deal. Quiet gulped the sherry down and smacked his lips. 'Ta.'

'I've got my eye on you,' Straw said.

Quiet just shrugged. 'Throat cut, then. That's how it was.'

'Like a second mouth,' Straw murmured. 'Horrible sight.'

He turned away and walked back to his warehouse. The Quiet Man watched him go, then turned and spat onto the ground, wiping a hand across his mouth and grimacing.

Chapter Nine

On a roof above Whitehall, hidden among the tall stacks of the brick chimneys, a small woman of about sixty years of age stood, scanning the grey skies above London with a pair of binoculars. She was dressed in a flapping trench-coat and heavy brogue shoes. Her hair, tied up inside a headscarf, was grey and wiry. A cigarette jutted from one corner of her mouth, and a thin, unbroken streamer of smoke curled up from the other.

This was Doctor 'Scobie' Beasley, expert in communications, and one of Whitehall's consultants on Soviet affairs.

Now she was impatient. And worried. The damned bird was over a day late, even allowing for its curious route between the two countries . . .

'Panama, where *are* you?' she murmured, and coughed as smoke went too deeply into her lungs.

Beside her, in four elegant coops, several birds watched her curiously, their voices mere gentle warblings, simple requests for food, flight and sex.

Behind her, then, the skylight window banged open. A portly man emerged, red-faced and panting. He wore a baggy pin-striped suit. His hair and moustaches were ginger, and he peered at Scobie through gold, half-framed glasses.

'Any sign?' he called breathlessly, and eased his bulk up off the ladder and on to the roof.

William Dugdale. A Whitehall Jack-of-all-Trades, but mostly a spy-catcher and a spy runner. He brushed himself down, then leaned forward and coughed for a moment or two, breathing deeply to return his strained bodily system to its normal functioning.

'Terrible climb,' he muttered. 'Why can't pigeons use basement doors . . .'

'Trouble with Panama,' Scobie called to him as he approached her, 'He likes the ladies. No sense of urgency.'

'Too many human agents like that,' Dugdale retorted. He stood and stared upwards. The sky, it seemed to him, was *full* of pigeons. How on earth could Doctor Beasley spot hers among so many?

He said, 'Pray that the bird hasn't gone astray. G.C.H.Q. has too much stuff on Murmansk. I really would like to read what Panama's got on the subject.'

'He'll be here,' Scobie murmured; then lowered her glasses, peeled the cigarette from her lip and looked at it with an expression of disgust. 'By the way, the Under Secretary phoned. Wanted to know where you were.'

'What did you tell him?'

She shrugged. 'Just that you were at an agent's funeral.'

Dugdale hovered about for a minute more, breathing the fresher air of the exposed rooftop, then he turned and went back to his suite of offices. His secretary, an attractive and efficient woman called Joanna Ross, was spreading out three files on his desk. She smiled as Dugdale entered.

'All marked urgent. Sorry. Just came down from room twelve.'

'Damn,' he said, taking off his jacket and walking round the desk. 'Joanna,' he went on, as he sat down, 'Doctor Beasley's getting awfully wrapped up in these damned pigeons. See if we can send her off for a bit of training. Karate, something like that.'

'You're joking!'

Dugdale chuckled. 'Of course I'm joking.' He grew solemn again, and stared distractedly out of the window. 'Poor old Anthony. A good man for such a rotten end. Nobody ought to have their throats cut these days. Umbrella needle, much more civilized.'

Joanna looked as glum as Dugdale felt. She'd liked Anthony Lacey as well. 'Was it the opposition?'

'A very nasty member *of* it. Most unpleasant.' He looked at the files, then sighed and pushed them away. 'What news from Manchester?'

She said, 'A stranger has turned up in the Operation Homer zone. Another tramp. They call him the Quiet Man, but he isn't known to our local boy.'

Dugdale digested that snippet of information. Tramps came and went wherever there was a sort of permanent hobo settlement. There was nothing unusual in that . . .

'Is that all?'

Joanna looked slightly solemn. 'Apparently he's asking about Anthony's murder.'

More interested, Dugdale sat up straighter. 'Is he now? Ask our people to try for a photograph. God knows they have enough expensive equipment . . . what's this?' He frowned as Joanna smiled and drew a ten by eight black and white photograph from the file she still carried. 'Ah,' Dugdale said. 'Apologies to North West Surveillance . . .' He turned the photograph and scrutinized it carefully.

And suddenly the familiar features of thc tramp seemed to emerge from behind the unfamiliar features of the disguise.

'Good Gordon Highlanders! Bloody Bulman!'

'I thought we knew the face,' Joanna said.

Dugdale stood up and pulled on his jacket. 'Get a car from the pool. Oh. And I need some sort of clock. That carriage clock in Beasley's room. Bring it to me, would you?'

'What for?'

'Our tramp is a clock mender.'

'Oh. Right. But the clock isn't broken.'

'It will be when you trip and drop it on the way back to me . . .'

*

Lucy was in the process of hanging up a framed print, in an attempt to brighten up the offce, when Dugdale opened the door of the shop and stepped inside. He unbuttoned his black overcoat, and looked around, clearly impressed with the look of the place, with its clocks, models, and polished furniture.

Lucy watched him suspiciously. He was quite unlike the usual sort of customer they entertained. He seemed too self-assured.

'Can I help you?'

Dugdale held out the clock, unwrapping it from its brown paper. 'I have this rather nice clock. Georgian, I believe.'

Lucy took the piece from him and inspected it. It was delicate and beautiful. She could go a long way to understanding Bulman's fascination with the things when she handled something this intricate. 'It's lovely,' she said.

'But unfortunately not working. It was dropped. Terrible accident . . .'

Lucy took it behind Bulman's desk and drew out his work ledger. 'If you'd like to leave it, we'll take a look.'

She began to write. She was still slightly suspicious of the ginger-haired man. He walked about the shop, staring closely at clocks, and prints, and making sounds that announced his pleasure at some of the items he saw.

'Is, um . . . is George around?'

'No. Would next week be all right?'

'I'm sorry?'

'For the clock. To collect it. Next week.'

'Oh, of course. Capital.'

He came over to the desk. Hands in his pockets, he stared at the girl, and Lucy felt distinctly uncomfortable. 'And your name?' she asked.

'Dugdale. William Dugdale.'

'Dugdale . . .' she repeated as she scribbled it down.

'George mentioned me, has he? Mentioned me to you?'

Lucy gave him her sternest stare, face quite devoid of expression. 'No.'

'We're old . . . old colleagues. From way back.'

Lucy placed the pen down and folded her arms. She had grasped what was going on now. 'You're job.'

'Job?'

'Policeman.'

Dugdale laughed. 'Policeman? Me? Oh good God, no.' He laughed again, then frowned and sort of shrugged. 'Well. In a way. Perhaps. That sort of thing.'

There was silence. Lucy said, 'Whitehall.'

'In a nutshell.'

'And you came all the way to Shanghai Road to get your clock fixed . . .'

Dugdale sat down on the chair across from Lucy. 'George Bulman is an expert. Tell me Miss McGinty . . .'

She was startled by his knowing her name.

'Where is he now?'

'On a case,' she said. 'And that's all I'm telling you. How do you know my name?'

Dugdale just smiled. 'Any chance of a cup of tea?'

'Not one in a million.'

'You've got your father's stubbornness.'

'You knew my father?'

'Very well indeed,' Dugdale said. 'I'd thought you were at Edinburgh University.'

'It was St Andrews,' Lucy said. She felt at a loss. She knew she was being manipulated, but she didn't know why or by whom. George had never mentioned a Dugdale, and nor had her father. And yet something about the man made her feel he was telling the truth.

'But when you heard that George Bulman, Detective Chief Inspector, had quit the Met you abandoned your studies and hot-footed it here, to London. In the blood, is it? Detective work?'

'Must be.'

Dugdale smiled. 'I was pleased to discover – when I checked you out, recently – that your partnership with

George is acquiring something of a . . . reputation, shall we say.'

Lucy leaned forward, pert face angry, but eyes giving away the fact that she was nervous. 'If it's to hire us that you want, we charge by the day, Mister Dugdale. With expenses extra. S.T.G. Investigations does not do divorce. Or credit inquiries.'

'But dear girl. I have the whole apparatus of the State at my fingertips. At a fraction, I suspect, of the cost.'

'And a fraction of the result,' Lucy retorted. 'Which is why you're here . . .'

Dugdale stiffened slightly, and some of the humour went from his face. The girl was confronting him, a sporty little type. Her eyes were fiery. When she was under pressure her Glasgow accent became more pronounced.

Speaking quietly, but now far more directly, Dugdale asked, 'Where is he?'

'I told you. Out of town.'

He fixed her with a hard gaze. He smiled very thinly, then shook his head. 'Some of my colleagues use threats. Seems shabby to me. But a business such as yours surely needs a degree of . . . laissez faire, shall we say. On the part of the authorities.'

'You play dirty,' Lucy said after a moment.

'Where is he?' Dugdale quietly persisted.

Sighing with resignation, Lucy sat back in her chair. 'He's living rough. Among some dossers . . . tramps.'

'Doing what precisely?'

'A murder. Investigating one.'

'Be more specific, girl. Which murder?'

'One the authorities had no real interest in. An old tramp. Called the Professor.'

'Well, well,' Dugdale said softly. 'How on earth did he get to hear about it, I wonder . . .'

'A retired priest came to see him. Desmond O'Dowd. I didn't want George to take the case. They only offered a hundred pounds. But George knew this Professor, apparently. Thought he was a nice chap. O'Dowd said that the police weren't interested. Probably another tramp did it, they reckoned. Influence of meths, or to steal his shoes. But O'Dowd thought it was more sinister, and only George could help. He talked him into it . . .'

'Heart of gold,' Dugdale said.

'Final demand for water rates, more like,' Lucy retorted. 'We're still eight quid short. We'd expected some reward money, but we nabbed the wrong villain.'

'How tragic.' Dugdale rose to his feet. 'I presume you have a line of communication?'

Lucy warily nodded. 'We keep in touch.'

'Then please tell George to get in contact with me soonest. Night or day. Thank you for your co-operation. Oh, and the clock job stands, if you wouldn't mind. Broke it rather too well.'

He walked from the shop, to the black limousine waiting outside for him.

Back at Whitehall, Dugdale walked quickly to his office, summoning Scobie Beasley on the way. He flung his scarf and hat into a corner, went round his desk and sat, muttering, 'Bulman, Bulman . . . God protect me from gumshoes with a nose for a problem.'

Scobie entered the office. She looked quite smart, having changed into a grey suit the moment she'd finished with roof duty. The cigarette still dangled from her mouth, however.

'Who's Bulman?'

'Bulman is what one might call the Random Factor. Also known as the Thorn in the Ointment . . .'

'Fly.'

Dugdale chuckled mirthlessly. 'There's nothing fly about Bulman. I know what I mean when I say "thorn". Anyway, give me the full update on Operation Homer.'

Scobie crossed to the pegboard screen and pinned up several items: a map of the Manchester docks area, an enlarged photograph of the Professor, now marked with a red cross, a photograph of Jack Straw, and a picture of a pigeon.

'I've now officially listed Panama as missing. That's a serious break in the comm-link. Anthony's death has been more than an inconvenience, I'm afraid. We've fielded young Fairbanks as a sort of long stop. But what we really need is a man in close . . .'

'Like at about silly mid off.'

'An impossible task . . .'

'I wouldn't be so sure,' Dugdale said, and chuckled quietly.

Scobie glared at him. 'I hope you're not playing someone from outside my team, Bill.'

Still chuckling, Dugdale said, 'Dear me no, Scobie. Heaven forfend. But let us say that a spectator has run onto the pitch. A useful spectator.'

'This Bulman?'

'Yes.'

The woman thought hard for a moment. 'P.I.'

'Yes.'

'How close has he come to the wicket?'

Dugdale steepled his fingers and stared at the pegboard. 'That, Doctor Beasley, is the question. But if I know George Bulman, he's got one finger on the bails already . . .'

Unaware that he was becoming an increasingly important topic of conversation in Whitehall, George Bulman – alias the Quiet Man – continued to cultivate a friendship with Rosy. Something about the old lady was not quite right. He remembered her from a few years before, although he'd hardly spoken to her then, and his professional opinion was that she was worried by something.

Something that was more than the death of her Professor.

Bulman was coming to the conclusion that Rosy held one, if not several, of the keys to the Professor's death.

He packed up his boxes and tied them together

before stacking them in the dry. He stretched and yawned. The life of a tramp was hard on his bones, and harder still on his stomach. This was the beginning of his third day here, and in that time he'd managed to eat decently just once. Inside his coat he had food supplies which he nibbled under cover of darkness, but he'd have given anything, right now, for one of Nicko's doner kebabs . . . or a pan full of mixed grill, the bacon cooked crisp, the eggs all runny.

He slapped himself out of the daydream of food, and ate two wholemeal biscuits. He had a pack of sausages, and he felt certain that it was time to eat them . . . it may have been cold *outside*, but inside his long overcoat the temperature was very high, and the sausages had begun to smell even through their cellophane.

He was the Quiet Man. He wouldn't have to explain where he'd got the meat. He'd just start frying them, this evening, using Rosy's battered old teflon saucepan, and the smell, and hunger, would be the answer to all suspicions.

Several of the group of tramps were crouched around the sprawled ashes of the fire. They hadn't got enough wood or firelighters to keep it going all day, so they were saving their fuel for dusk, and the real cold.

Rosy herself was standing apart from the group, her pram by her side and the dog sitting by the pram, licking its forepaws. She was gazing out over the water, to the far side of the canal, and the industrial area there, where already lorries moved.

Bulman walked up to her. 'Thought you was moving on, Rosy.'

She shrugged. Without smiling, without looking at him, she said, 'No rush.'

She was lost, Bulman thought. For the first time in years she didn't have the Professor to lead the way, or give her a reassuring bit of waffle.

'Miss 'im, do you?' Bulman asked gently.

'He was good to me, Quiet. Not like the other ones. Bastards.'

The dog panted, looking up at Bulman. It extended a paw, wrapped in a grimy bandage. Bulman smiled at it.

Rosy said, 'Coppers was down. Asked me a lot of questions. But they didn't care. Just a tramp, wasn't he. Which one did it, they kept saying. Was it meths? A binge? Bit of an argument? They wouldn't have hardly cared if we'd *all* done it. They kept laughing.'

'What'd you tell them?'

Rosy looked around at him, her face, behind the dirt, sorrowful. 'You got any more smokes?'

'Nary a one. Sorry, Rosy.' He looked towards the dead fire. 'Ought to make it up. Going to be a cold day.'

Rosy said, 'Reckon I'll push on to Lincoln.'

'Why Lincoln?'

'They got proper places, there. More tolerant of people like us. So I've heard.' She looked at Bulman again, her eyes watery. 'They asked if he had enemies.'

'Did he?'

'I expect so. There ain't nobody here without them.'

She sniffed loudly, wiped a sleeve across her nose, then rattled the pram, a gesture of growing frustration.

Bulman murmured, 'He who has a thousand friends, has not an enemy to spare . . .'

Rosy chuckled, shaking her head. 'You an' Bernard would've got on a treat.'

'We did,' Bulman said. 'How long had he been on the road, you reckon?'

'Oh . . . off and on. Years, I suppose. Four years wiv me . . . 'E were a teacher once, you know. He used to tell lovely stories.'

'Did he go down the steps often? The wharf steps. Where he was found . . .'

Rosy thought about that. 'Yeah. I suppose he did. 'E had a friend. Wiv a boat.'

'What sort of boat?'

'Ordinary sort. Wooden job, wiv oars. They use 'em for working around the water. Just a boat . . .'

The dog suddenly barked, and both Bulman and Rosy glanced round. Jack Straw stood a few feet away, staring at them.

Rosy seemed to get upset. 'Gotta be getting on,' she said, and started to push the pram away from the water's edge. She went back towards the fire, still dreaming of Lincoln.

Bulman ignored the weasly little man as he walked over to the side of the canal. 'It's a shame about the old man,' Straw said. Bulman made no response. Straw went on, 'I don't suppose anyone could take his place . . .'

Puzzled, Bulman tried to hide that feeling by answering in a deadpan voice, 'Take 'is place doing what?'

'Whatever it was he was up to,' Jack Straw said evenly, and walked away from Bulman. Bulman watched him go.

What was all that about?

He fumbled inside his coat, and his hand came to rest on the cool metal of his opera glasses. He looked around, sought out a nice vantage point.

Saw it.

Walked slowly round the wasteland, until he could climb in relative obscurity . . .

Watching from his bird house, Jack Straw saw Selwyn's green Bedford van drive slowly to the edge of the deserted wharf. It stopped where it always stopped, by the overgrown railway tracks that ran around the edge of the complex of rusting sheds and crumbling warehouses. Selwyn, a chubby man in a leather jacket, did what he always did. He stepped out of the van and lounged on the pile of old railway sleepers, reading the *Sun* and chewing his way through a kebab.

After a few minutes he folded the newspaper, stuck the remains of the pitta bread into the wrapping paper, and tossed it over his shoulder.

Then he went back to his van and drove off.

Straw waited until this moment, even though there

was always the risk that one of the tramps would see the discarded food and go for it. He clambered down the ladder to the warehouse's first landing, then down the stairs to the ground. He walked briskly to the grass-covered railway line and picked up the litter.

Inside the corner piece of bread was a small black tube.

Back in his pigeon loft, Straw attached the tube to Panama's leg. The bird cooed gently, watching him with its bright, unblinking eyes.

'A long wait, young Panama. But I couldn't help it. If anyone down at Whitehall asks . . . just tell 'em you met this smashing bird . . .'

With the message tube secure, he opened the skylight and flung the bird upwards. The pigeon flapped noisily for a moment, circled once about the building, then winged off south.

'Safe journey, my lovely,' Straw whispered, then closed the skylight.

A quarter of a mile away, stretched out on the roof of another warehouse, George Bulman frowned and lowered his opera glasses. He watched the pigeon as it winged away towards London; when it was out of sight he returned his gaze to the open loading bay where he could just see Jack Straw moving about.

And nothing made any sense at all.

Chapter Ten

Day four began with gnawing, intolerable hunger. Bulman almost kicked off his boxes. He was going through the worst agony he had known in years, and all for a favour, and a hundred pounds.

O'Dowd was asking too much. He could understand why Desmond O'Dowd would want to see justice done for the old Professor, and he sympathized with the sentiment himself. But this cold, this hunger . . .

Was it worth it, he asked himself.

There was a fire going, and someone had brewed some tea. He sipped his portion and thought of the lovely cuppa he might have been having in the Shanghai Road. But the hot fluid warmed him, and he ate some biscuits, and soon cheered up.

Then he remembered what day this was. They would all trek to the outskirts of the town, and find the Hope Mission. There, in exchange for a sing song, they would be rewarded with soup.

It would be a chance to speak to O'Dowd. And a chance to stock up with consumables.

By one o'clock the mission was almost full, more than eighty down-and-outs from all over the area. They crowded around the tables, singing at the tops of their voices, some even banging their tin soup mugs in rhythm to the organ music that O'Dowd was pushing out.

In the middle of the smelly throng, Bulman sang at the peak of his ability. He was quite enjoying himself. He had pockets full of cooked chicken and bacon – although only just: the butcher hadn't let him into the shop, but agreed to serve him outside!

When Jack Straw came into the mission, and took his place among the tramps, he saw Bulman but avoided his eyes. Somehow the little bird man seemed out of place . . . both here, *and* in his castle by the canal . . .

The music ended. O'Dowd thanked everyone for their singing, reminded them that he was there as a spiritual and religious adviser, then declared the soup hatch open. There was a veritable stampede towards the two beaming women who ladled the broth into cups and passed out the bread.

Bulman remained seated. Straw joined the queue and was pushed out of eyeshot. Green Hat, sitting next to Bulman, hesitated, but when Bulman told him to go and fetch his soup he went gratefully.

O'Dowd came over, sat down opposite Bulman and began to talk in an easy whisper. 'Any luck?'

'There's something bloody odd going on,' Bulman said. 'Begging your pardon, Father.'

O'Dowd smiled. 'I'm no longer "Father", I've told you that. They took it all away from me. Stripped of my priestly honours.'

'What was it?' Bulman asked. 'Saying the Latin Mass?'

'Breaking the vows of chastity.'

Bulman couldn't help a grin. O'Dowd looked less amused.

'That bloke, Jack Straw . . .' Bulman asked.

'An enigma. I don't know much about him. He seems wrong somehow.'

'My thoughts exactly. How did he and the Professor get on?'

O'Dowd leaned forward slightly, glancing around. The tables were filling up, and the air filled with chatter and the clatter of spoons on tin. 'Very much the same as you and he get on. He's an odd one. Keeps pigeons. Wild pigeons . . .'

Bulman nodded. 'He's chary of me because I'm going about asking questions. Two or three days isn't long enough to use much finesse.'

Straw sat down close by, immersed himself in the

task of eating. But Bulman was uncannily aware that he was being kept an eye on.

'Better get some soup,' Bulman said. His knee was irritating him. Couldn't think why. Something that O'Dowd had said, maybe . . .

When he'd finished eating, Jack Straw left the mission as silently and uncommunicatively as he had come. Bulman followed him outside and saw him walking briskly in the direction of the town.

This was his chance. The chance to check out Jack Straw's castle . . .

He walked quickly back to the warehouse. There was no one about, of course, they were all too busy queuing for seconds at the Hope Mission. Bulman hadn't expected to find the front entrance locked, but it was. He had to climb to a broken window and edge his way inside onto the first floor. Stairs led up from the litter-strewn space, and he mounted them nervously to the trap door which led into the pigeon loft itself.

The place stank of birds. The walls were coated with white droppings, and free pigeons shuffled restlessly about in the open entrance of the loading bay.

There were several cages, however, covered by a tarpaulin. Bulman lifted this away and inspected the birds within. These were no wild pigeons, not by a long shot. Two of the cages were empty. He checked those first, searching for something, anything, that might give a clue as to what Jack Straw's game was.

He found nothing. Careful not to loose the birds themselves, he checked the inhabited cages, then covered them with the tarpaulin again.

'It's all got to mean something, darlings . . .' he said loudly to his feathered observers. The birds fluttered restlessly. Outside, he heard the raised voice of one of the tramps. Peering out he saw Rosy and Green Hat walking slowly back to the dead fire. To his surprise he found his heart was beating rather fast.

He didn't want to get caught on Straw's property. Not yet.

But just as he made to leave the loading bay he saw the green van again. He drew back and watched from the shadows. The van parked where it had parked yesterday, and the same chubby man stepped out, a paper under his arm, and sat down by the black wooden sleepers of the disused railway.

He began to unwrap a pack of sandwiches.

He glanced quickly up at the warehouse, then opened the paper and began to read.

She was hungry. The thought of egg and chips at Nicko's was most enticing. At one o'clock in the afternoon Lucy gave up the waiting game and abandoned herself to the demands of her stomach.

Just as she reached the door a thought occurred to her. Maybe George was so far from a phone that he had had no way of contacting her. Maybe he *wasn't* just leaving her in the dark out of spite . . .

She hadn't *meant* to object to him taking the case. It was just that they were so hard up at the moment, what with Greenstein turning the tables on them, and the American bank refusing to pay expenses . . .

When the priest – the ex-priest, she should have said – had come with his tale of hobo-woe, it had seemed just the wrong break for S.T.G. Investigations.

She shouldn't have been so surly with George. She felt guilty, now, and very sorry.

But he should have phoned in at least *once* in four days!

She walked back to the answering machine and flicked out the tiny tape spool. Maybe . . . maybe she should leave the message for *George*.

Good idea. She re-recorded the message, asking callers to leave their names and numbers, and then added at the end, 'George, the ginger moustache wants to talk to you. Urgent.'

Maybe he'd call, get the message, and at least he would know that Dugdale was on his case.

She went back to the door, stepped outside and locked up.

'Miss McGinty?'

Turning round she found herself facing one of the most beautiful men she had ever seen. He was tall, fair, and grey eyed. He was young and slim, and impeccably dressed in a grey tweed suit. His smile was easy, his manner self-assured. Behind him his car was a steel grey Metro, not exactly class, but it gleamed with confidence.

'Yes. I am . . .' she said. The young man gave a little bow.

'Nice to meet you. I'm Peter Ripley. I work for the man who brought the clock in . . . ?'

'It's not ready . . .' Lucy managed to say.

'That's fine. In fact, Mister Dugdale has asked me to invite you to his office. I've brought the car.'

'No thanks,' Lucy said. Ripley looked a little crest-fallen, but the easy smile remained on his lips.

'It really won't take long,' he said, his voice a clear attempt to charm her. And why not? There was little enough of it about.

'I'm off to lunch.'

'Whitehall lunches are terrible,' Ripley said. 'But I'll fetch you in anything you like.'

She hesitated. She liked him. Maybe Whitehall wasn't so bad after all. 'A fillet steak, very rare, between two crusts of granary bread.'

Ripley laughed. 'It shall be yours. I might have one too . . .'

Lucy looked at him, still unsure. 'Is it really important?'

'I wouldn't be here if it wasn't. We think your partner could be in danger, and perhaps it's time you knew why . . .'

'Who's we?'

'Mister Dugdale and myself.'

'The Funny People.'

'I'm the straight man. Will you come?'

'Of course,' she said. She followed him into the Metro.

They went more or less straight to Whitehall, stopping only so that Peter Ripley could buy two steaks at a local butchers. He winked at Lucy as he climbed back into the car. 'This could start a precedent. I approve.'

Dugdale, too, was as charming as he had been the time before. He sat Lucy down, supplied her with some Ministry tea, and watched in silent admiration as her steak roll was brought in, and wolfishly consumed before his very eyes.

Then they talked.

'What I really have to know – in some detail, my dear – is precisely what has taken George Bulman down among the hoboes, like some character from one of those incomprehensible films by Luis Bunuel.'

'Just what I told you,' she said evenly. 'He's investigating a murder.'

'And has he phoned in?'

'If he had, I would have passed on your request. But he hasn't. So I haven't.'

'And it was the unfrocked priest who asked him.'

'Yes. O'Dowd.'

'Simply out of conscience. Out of the love of Homo Hobolis.'

'Is that a joke?'

'Apparently not.'

The door opened and Doctor Beasley entered. She hesitated as she saw Lucy, but Dugdale called her in. She crossed to the desk and placed a file, open, in front of him. They exchanged a look and a smile.

'I'm so glad . . .' Dugdale said.

'Me too,' the woman said. 'I wondered if a hawk had got him. Or one of those dreadful children with an air rifle.'

Dugdale scanned the writing on the page, then nodded. 'This is damned useful. Well done, Scobie.' He looked up at the older woman. 'Feel up to a little seminar? For Miss McGinty, here?'

'If you like . . .'

Dugdale stared at Lucy, then patted the file. 'One of our agents just reported home safely. We thought he'd got lost.'

Lucy just smiled, not knowing whether or not she was expected to speak.

After a moment's thoughtful silence, Dugdale went on, 'Have you ever signed the Official Secrets Act?'

'No,' she said. 'And I don't intend to.'

'Oh dear,' Dugdale murmured. But he brightened. 'So if I let you into a secret, you'll at least behave responsibly.'

'If it has to do with George, of course I will.'

'Hmm.' Dugdale assessed her for a few seconds, then came to a decision. 'Right. To the briefing room. Scobie, get your slides. This young woman is about to learn something of the sophisticated art of PanGlobal Communication.'

The briefing room was a small, dimly-lit cubbyhole, about a hundred paces from Dugdale's office, but reached by a system of winding stairs, double doors and featureless passageways. Once inside, Lucy was directed to one of the ten, hard chairs, and Scobie Beasley began to load slides into a carousel. She smoked heavily as she worked and talked, and Lucy began to feel slightly sick as the atmosphere thickened.

'Knew a McGinty once,' Scobie said, coughing as she spoke. 'A detective. Very good man.'

'My father,' Lucy said, and the woman looked surprised, then impressed. 'Well well.'

'And here we are,' Dugdale appended, giving Lucy a gentle, and friendly pat on the shoulder. 'The next generation.'

When the slides were loaded and ready, Scobie stubbed out her cigarette, but immediately drew another one from a black carton. She walked to the screen at the front of the room and picked up the remote control system, flicking through until a slide that showed just the words OPERATION HOMER appeared before Lucy.

Then she turned to the dim room. 'Bill. What degree of frankness is expected here?'

Dugdale thought hard for a moment, half glancing at Lucy. 'You can speak with complete freedom. Up to Secret. And limited to the subject of Homer. If you have to say more, I'll say it for you.'

Lucy felt as if she was a naughty child, being let into certain secrets but not others. It made her blood boil slightly. She hated not to be trusted when she was so trustworthy.

The next slide came into view. It showed a pigeon just about to land, wings spread and feathered, head turned slightly as it recoiled from the shutter sound of the camera that was capturing the image.

Drily, Lucy said, 'Don't tell me this is one of your agents . . .'

With a sour smile, Scobie Beasley said to Dugdale, 'I told you she was an astute little number, Bill. Yes, dear,' she said to Lucy. 'This is Panama. Handsome chap, isn't he? You'll meet the real thing in a moment. Fifteen ounces of flesh, feather . . . and true grit. We thought he'd defected, but he just came home . . .'

'A pigeon!' Lucy said in some astonishment.

Dugdale and Scobie exchanged a look, and Dugdale murmured, 'No slouch in ornithology.'

'I don't believe this.'

The next slide flickered up. It showed a map of Northern Europe and the Soviet Union.

Scobie lit her cigarette, puffed for a couple of seconds, then started to talk, almost reflectively. 'Pulp fiction, and the popular press, have built up a picture of intelligence gathering being conducted from satellites in orbit, and from radio eavesdropping by spy planes, and all sorts of electronic surveillance. The days, we are now told, of "cold war" back alleys, spies coming in from the cold, and cat burglars in submarine pens are gone. Finished. Old fashioned.'

Dugdale turned in his chair and chuckled as he faced Lucy. 'Which is a lot of baloney,' he said. 'They've never gone away. In fact, they're the main *modus operandi* of the cold war *still*. More and more electronic gadgetry means less and less security . . . of communications, for instance.'

Scobie added, 'Particularly from inside unfriendly territory.'

Lucy looked from one to the other of them. 'And you still use pigeons?'

Dugdale shrugged. 'Never stopped. Been using 'em since Roman times.'

The slide showed Panama again, and Scobie said, 'And this young fellah has been playing a particularly interesting game with us.'

'What game . . .?'

Dugdale chuckled. 'Panama is the first known instance of a pigeon who's turned into a double agent!'

'A pigeon!' Lucy said, her voice almost shrill with astonishment. 'A double agent?'

Dugdale patted her hand. 'Calm down, Lucy. You've not heard anything yet . . .'

Nothing was fitting together. Or if it was, the tribulations of his adopted role were confusing his thought processes, and he wasn't seeing the obvious.

Bulman rearranged everything in Straw's pad so that there would be no sign of his visit, then he descended the steps, and the stairs, to the chill outside world. Rosy was pushing her pram, and tugging at the dog. She looked lost, and very concerned. Her action was a sort of aimless ramble, and Bulman caught her up and strolled along with her.

'Thought you was off to Lincoln,' he said.

Rosy remained silent, not greeting him, not looking at him.

Bulman persisted, 'What'll you do there? Lincoln.'

She shrugged. Then she stopped pushing the pram

and turned to her new friend. There were tears in her eyes. The dirt on the skin of her cheeks was smeared.

'I miss 'im, Quiet. It's getting worse.'

'I know you do,' Bulman said softly. 'But the pain'll go . . .'

'Know wot 'e said? Before it happened . . .'

'What was that, Rosy?'

' 'E said if I went to Lincoln 'e wouldn't come wiv me.'

'He wouldn't?'

'Said 'e *couldn't*. He *couldn't* come to Lincoln. I'd 'ave to go on my own.'

Bulman was thoughtful for a moment. Rosy began to push her pram again, and Bulman fell into step beside her. 'There's a world of difference. A lot of difference.'

She sniffed and glanced at him. 'What's that mean?'

'Well . . . if he *wouldn't* come with you, that means he didn't want to. But if he *couldn't* come with you, that means there was reasons. Something was keeping him from leaving here . . .'

There was a long silence. Rosy sniffed more loudly and drew a sleeve across her nose. She stopped the pram. Frowning, she looked up at the Quiet Man. 'I thought 'e were fond of me.'

'Well, he was,' Bulman pointed out. 'He spoke to me about you. Years ago. When I was down these parts. Come on, Rosy, you *do* remember me, don't you?'

She smiled a little. 'Course I do.'

She had probably recognized him from the moment he'd turned up on the dockside.

'He was a kind man,' Bulman said.

'He led me on. I thought . . . I really thought . . .'

'Thought what?'

She shrugged, shook her head.

'You thought he'd go to Lincoln with you. You thought you were that close. Well, you were, Rosy. You got to believe that.'

Again they walked. Bulman asked, 'Anyway, what's so special about Lincoln?'

'It's tidy there,' the woman said. 'And they welcome people like us. So I've 'eard.'

Bulman couldn't help smiling. Dreams of streets paved with gold. Where had he heard that before? He stopped and watched as Rosy walked sadly on. His knee was irritating him. He turned and looked up at Straw's castle.

He began to understand . . .

'In every sense of the word,' Scobie said, 'Panama is an agent. We field a lot of agents as couriers, or runners, and that's precisely what Panama does . . .'

The screen showed the fourth view of the pigeon, and even Dugdale was rather restless with Scobie Beasley's passion for pictures of the bird.

He turned to Lucy again. 'The pigeon flies regularly here from a submarine base in north-west Russia.'

That meant something to Lucy. 'Murmansk?' she volunteered.

Scobie beamed. 'Isn't she bright? Her father's daughter. Yes, that's exactly right. Murmansk . . .'

Dugdale went on, 'The K.G.B. have an agent in Manchester Docks. He's an ex-safe cracker who offered his services to the Communists here.'

Scobie sneered. 'A *dreadful* safe cracker, my dear. But he certainly knows his pigeons.'

'True enough,' Dougdale said. 'He breeds them. Dear old Jack Straw could write a book on pigeons. Wouldn't be as good as Scobie here's book, of course . . .'

Scobie smiled at that. 'Anyway,' she said, 'Using means that I . . . er . . .'

'Can't reveal,' Dougdale finished for her.

'Using means that I can't reveal – but Straw's a clever bastard, all right – he worked out a system whereby he could lure our pigeons . . . *trick* our pigeons, really . . . into making a stopover at Manchester, en route from Murmansk to London.'

'The purpose being . . .?'

'To remove a message tube from its leg.' Scobie reached into her skirt pocket and drew out a small black tube. 'Just like this one. Inside, coded information from our agent in Murmansk. The purpose of the intercept is for the K.G.B. in Manchester to get a first look at what's coming through.'

'*And,*' Dugdale interrupted, with a hint of excitement in his voice, 'To doctor it. To mislead us.'

Lucy couldn't quite understand why they seemed so pleased with an operation that was clearly so inefficient. She said, 'So the pigeon method is insecure . . .'

'Precisely,' Scobie said. 'Isn't that clever?'

Dugdale put her out of her misery. 'You see, we get the real stuff from highly secret satellite communications. The great usefulness of Panama, and his father, and his grandfather . . . indeed, *all* his family, is that we give the K.G.B. a chance to let us read the signals as they would *prefer* us to have them.'

Light dawned. Understanding came. Lucy's eyes widened as she registered how impressed she was by Homer's cleverness. 'I've got it! That way you can gauge what is important to them. Feed them stuff from our agent in Murmansk to let them think you know less, or more, than you do.'

'Precisely,' Scobie said. 'It's an excellent game.' She held up the black tube again. 'This is the next move. It'll fly to Murmansk on Santiago, Panama's son. Via Manchester, of course. Santiago is another handsome chap, a little cocky, perhaps.'

Dugdale muttered something under his breath. Lucy thought it might have been: *we've got to get you off these damn birds . . .* She asked, aloud, 'What about the Professor? He seems to be the link in *two* games.'

Dugdale said, 'The Professor was with this department. He was keeping an eye on Jack Straw and his K.G.B. contact. Chap with a photography business in Manchester.'

'And they found out about him and cut his throat.'

'We're not sure,' Scobie said. 'That's actually where your man in the field could be of some assistance.'

Dugdale added, 'George could also be in very grave danger.'

'Yes,' Lucy said. 'I can understand.'

'We really do need to know,' he went on, 'If the *other* side murdered poor Anthony. The Professor. Or was it simply a by-product of his life undercover?'

'How long had he been living like that?'

'Four years,' Scobie said, sitting down across one of the chairs and lighting another cigarette. 'Of course he surfaced for baths. De-briefing. Planning sessions. But the problem with living a cover is that one gets . . . involved. With all the peripheral stuff. Meths. Misery. Desperate need for survival. It could simply have been another tramp . . .'

They all stood and left the briefing room. Dougdale said, 'I'm sending you to the area. With Peter Ripley, the young man who shared your extravagant lunch. You'll look like water-workers, and you can try and make contact with George.'

He smiled, adding, 'And give him my regards.'

Chapter Eleven

Damn! Bulman thought vehemently. *Damn and double damn.*

He walked slowly away from the gathered group of tramps, shuffling slightly so that he didn't look too much in a hurry, and soon was out of sight. There were about twenty down-and-outs in the dock area, now, and many of them were winos, and were stinking drunk. Rosy regarded them with disgust. It would be the factor that really *did* set her moving on.

Damn, Bulman thought again.

It was after three o'clock. It was time to check in with Lucy and see if anything had turned up at her end. He had left it too long, but to go to a phone was risky. Several of the tramps had a lot more going for them than most, and were keeping a strict eye on the Quiet Man.

Bulman didn't fit. Every hour his cover grew weaker.

There was more than a murder going on here, he knew that now, but quite what it was he couldn't say. It wasn't his business, anyhow. He had been brought here by the retired priest to avenge the death of a tramp. Such vengeance now seemed quite pointless.

The sky was grey and miserable, rather like Bulman felt. He wanted to be back at the Shanghai Road, working on a clock, eating one of Nicko's kebabs. He wanted warmth and Lucy's chirpy voice nattering on to him.

He wasn't to know that at that moment Lucy, with one of Dugdale's men, was already passing Birmingham on the M6 motorway, the needle of the Ford Escort touching the hundred mark.

Beyond the clustered shells of the warehouses, beyond the deserted railway yard, beyond the high, glass-topped wall that seemed to stretch for miles, was a grey road that led towards the Mission, and then the outskirts of the town. There was a phone box here, an ordinary coin box, and Bulman fumbled in his inner belt for the appropriate number of ten-penny pieces.

He dialled the shop's number in London and waited for Lucy's voice to answer. When it did, and he had pressed in the first coin, he found to his irritation that she had set the answering machine going.

He almost hung up in disgust. But he didn't . . .

He was smiling grimly as he made his second call.

Should have bloody known! Staring me in the face all the bleedin' time!

When the phone was answered he asked for a certain extension. When the extension was answered he asked for Mister William Dugdale. He got the usual response from the secretary, that Mister Dugdale was in conference. And he smiled again.

'Just tell him it's George Bulman.'

'George Bulman?'

And a moment later – after the expected silence while Dugdale levered himself from sleep to attention – he heard the familiar rasping tones of his old Intelligence colleague.

'Dear boy!' Dugdale enthused. 'And how is life in the underworld? In its Orphean sense, I mean.'

'Why am I not stunned to learn that you know where I am, and doubtless what I'm doing?' Bulman asked, shaking his head as he looked along the road both ways.

Dugdale chuckled. 'For the same reason, dear boy, that I experienced a sensation of déjà vu when I spotted a surveillance photo of you dressed somewhat smarter than is your habit. I really must get the name of your tailor.'

Bulman smiled at the joke.

'Yeah. Okay, cutting corners then, does your office have a certain interest in a certain variety of our little feathered friends . . .'

'Affirmative,' Dugdale announced.

'Thought so. What about a chap called J.S.?'

'Other team,' Dugdale said, his voice a little lower.

'Right. Now listen carefully. I was down here on a case for a client, when this caper what you're involved in sort of starts to merge with mine . . .'

'George,' Dugdale interrupted. 'Say no more on the phone.'

'You'd better send somebody to meet me. There's a serious development. On the plus side.'

'It's all in hand,' Dugdale said. 'One of our best young men, and your best young woman, are even now winging through the Pennines to your relief . . . Hang up, dear boy. And stay on your usual patch.'

Bulman did so. As he stepped from the box he saw Desmond O'Dowd come cycling towards him, presumably to see who was available around the derelict wharf to recruit to his evening sing and soup session.

He dismounted, and skidded to a stop by Bulman. Behind him, the green van that was so often to be seen by the quay, drove across the intersection of two roads. Bulman noted it, but didn't refer to it.

O'Dowd glanced at the phone box. 'Checking in with Lucy, were you?'

'Yeah. Just routine.'

'Any closer?'

Bulman stared at the unshaven man, trying to imagine him as a priest. Listening to confessions, celebrating the Mass. He looked for all the world like one of his hobo clients.

'I don't know, Desmond. Listen, it could be any of them. Right?'

'Including me?'

Bulman shrugged, then shook his head. 'I'm getting there, Desmond. I'm getting close. No need for you to cancel the milk and papers I shouldn't think.'

'Well. That's a relief . . .'

O'Dowd mounted his bicycle again, and pedalled

off. As Bulman shuffled back towards the quay, the green van sidled across the intersection again.

Without slowing his pace, keeping his shuffle going, Bulman walked towards it. He was aware that the plump man was staring at him from the driver's cab. After a moment the van drove off.

Lucy and Dugdale's field man, Peter Ripley, arrived in the harbour area at just before five thirty in the afternoon. They parked the car, then Lucy tugged on a pair of paint-stained overalls. She tied her hair into a scarf and slung a canvas holdall over her shoulder. Ripley was dressed in green overalls and a woollen cap.

Across the water from them was a vast expanse of dereliction. It seemed to stretch for miles along the canal, and river side; smoke rose from several points in the grey wasteland, and even from this distance it was possible to see the shapes of people, dark people, shambling and shuffling as they grubbed for wood and paper for their fires.

'The whole area has been taken over,' Ripley said. 'There are more than a hundred tramps, formed into about twenty encampments. It's like a city. But a very grim city.'

'And somewhere among them is George . . . How do we get across?'

Ripley glanced about. 'Easiest way would be by boat. We can go down to the Hope Mission and ask your client where Bulman is to be located.'

They walked for a few minutes, and eventually found a small rowing boat that looked reasonably river-worthy. Nobody challenged them when they took it, and Ripley rowed quite strongly – he was an ex-Oxford man – and covered the water in no time at all.

They found the road that led to the Mission, and at the Mission found O'Dowd, doing some exterior painting. He seemed surprised to see Lucy, and stepped down the ladder, wiping his hands on a cloth.

'Lucy! I thought you were in London . . .'

'We're looking for George.'

'Are you . . .' O'Dowd looked at Ripley and smiled thinly. 'Another job come up?'

'Another job?' She grasped what he meant. 'Oh. No. This is one of our team.'

The two men exchanged a nod of acknowledgement.

'Do you know where George *is*?'

'Last I saw of him he was on the phone to you. That was a couple of hours ago.' O'Dowd seemed suspicious. Lucy just shrugged.

'Must have been talking to the answering machine.'

The priest glanced round, then pointed into the distance. 'George is with the group that camps at the base of that tall warehouse. See it? Shouldn't be hard to spot. Look for a woman with a pram and a dog. She's with the same group.'

'Right. Thanks.'

Lucy led the way from the Mission towards the place of tramps.

For a while Bulman watched Rosy from a short distance away. She had unpacked her pram, laying everything out neatly on the ground beside it. Now she contemplated her collection and slowly, almost lovingly, began to place the shoes and other objects back.

It was almost a daily ritual with her. It gave her something to do, and it was a perfect way to delay the moment of her departure. All her life on the road Rosy had been heading off somewhere else. She made her decision, then repacked the pram. When the packing was done she stayed where she was, until one day she thought: time to move on. And the whole process began again.

There was a small fire burning next to her. Bulman walked over, pulling his small, battered frying pan from his coat pocket. It was only an omelette pan, and most dossers carried one. He squatted down by the fire and started to cook two sausages, holding them above the flame until they gave up some of their fat.

'Where you off to today, Rosy?' he asked as the sausages began to sizzle. The dog looked up, then squirmed closer to the smell, its mouth open, its eyes wide with expectation.

'I reckon Doncaster. They say it's nice there.' She packed and shuffled, inspecting each shoe as she picked it up.

'What happened to Lincoln?'

'Gone off the idea of Lincoln. Doncaster's tidy. Not like this place . . .' She glanced around, an expression of disgust on her face. Then she looked down at Bulman, and at the cooking. 'Where'd you get them, then?'

'The priest. One's for you.'

She looked startled. She came away from the pram and squatted down next to him, watching the browning sausages, and occasionally looking at the Quiet Man.

'Why'd you give me one of them?'

'Because I likes yuh,' Bulman said, smiling. He shook the pan. The meat spluttered. 'Nearly done.'

Rosy stared at him. 'Me?'

'Me what?'

'You like me, Quiet?'

'Course I do, Rosy. Always have.'

They sat in silence until the sausages were cooked. Then Bulman reached in and plucked the plumpest of them out and passed it to the woman. 'There you go, Rosy. Careful. Hot.'

She took it, fumbled with it, then broke a piece off and gave it to the dog. The rest she pushed into her own mouth and began to chew vigorously.

'Ta, Quiet,' she murmured through her chewing. 'Yer a toff.'

Bulman ate in silence. He watched the woman. When the meat was down, and she was licking her fingers, he said, 'I guess you probably remember what happened, now. Do you?'

Rosy hesitated, then licked on. When she'd finished she didn't look at Bulman, but she nodded. 'Yeah.'

'What was it? A tiff?'

' 'E wouldn't come to Lincoln. I begged him. But he wouldn't come. And he said I wouldn't leave anyway. Said I was always talking about it and never did it.'

'That was unkind.'

'Said I'd never have the bottle to leave this . . . tip. We 'ad a bad row about it.' She was silent for a moment, still staring at the fire. 'Then 'e said my collection was rubbish.'

'Your collection . . .'

She looked up sharply. 'Me shoes.'

Silence. Then Bulman said, 'So you killed 'im.'

With a little sigh, and a look on her face that might almost have been wistful, she nodded. 'That's wot I done time for before. Murder.'

'I know,' Bulman said. 'I found out . . .'

'Will they lock me away?'

Reaching out, Bulman took her hand and squeezed it. She was icy cold. Her hand trembled. 'They'll take care of you, Rosy. Take care of you kindly . . .'

Her nod was a gesture of resignation. She drew a deep breath and looked round at her shoes, knowing that she'd probably not see them again. 'I'm sorry I done it.'

Knowing that the police would want a murder weapon, he asked carefully, 'What did you use, Rosy? Knife was it? Bit of tin?'

She frowned as she looked at him. 'What for?'

'You know. When you . . . when you cut 'is throat . . .'

'Cut 'is . . . ? What you saying, Quiet? You stupid, or something? Nah, I *nutted* him . . .' As she spoke she jerked her head forward. 'Like that. We was on the side there an' he fell in the water. Current got 'im. Washed up the next day, over by the steps.'

Bulman just watched her. She didn't know! She hadn't seen the body, just been told it was her beloved Professor. She didn't know *how* he'd been killed.

Well I'm damned!

There was movement behind him, which startled him. He turned and looked up. Lucy stood there, smiling down at his grimy features. A young man was with her, dressed scruffily but with all the bearing and facial appearance of one of Whitehall's finest.

'Blimey,' he said. 'That was quick.'

'Hello, Georgie,' Lucy said with a smile. Then she glanced at the sad figure of Rosy. 'Have you found what you were looking for?'

Bulman eased himself to his feet and shook his head. 'I thought I had. I really did. But I haven't.'

Rosy said plaintively, 'Will I have to go to prison?'

'You didn't kill him, love,' Bulman said loudly to her. The dog wagged its tail as if sensing the joy behind the words. 'You could've. But you didn't. You can go to Doncaster whenever you like, and no one's going to stop you.'

Rosy didn't say anything. She just stared up at him in wonderment.

It was all over for Jack Straw. He must have known it from the moment he saw the two new arrivals talking with the Quiet Man. Some villains might have run. But Straw was too old, too tired, too sensible.

He wouldn't have got very far.

He stood in the loading bay and watched as Quiet led the other two towards his home. As they vanished into the lower floor and began to climb the stairs, Straw looked around for the last time at the place that he had come to love.

When Bulman – acting with supreme caution – pushed open the trap door, Jack Straw was wishing a fond farewell to his favourite pigeon. He didn't look up as the three figures climbed in turn into the loft.

Only when Peter Ripley said, 'Mister Straw . . .?' did he turn towards them,

'Just a minute . . .'

He crossed to the open loading bay. He kissed the bird, then flung it high into the air. He stood watching it until it was out of sight.

Bulman and Lucy left Ripley to do the formal business of notification of rights, and arrest. And the less formal business of finding out exactly what the K.G.B. contact was up to next.

They sat on one of the empty hutches, out of earshot. Bulman peeled off his gloves and balaclava, and scratched inside his shirt. The aroma of his sweat was quite overpowering and Lucy, with a cheeky smile, shuffled a few inches away from him.

Quickly, then, she filled Bulman in on the whole operation. Pigeon power. Panama flying from East to West, and Santiago flying West to East.

Santiago was expected at any time . . . the final evidence that Jack Straw was working for the K.G.B.

'What'll happen to him?' Lucy asked, when the briefing was finished. Straw and Ripley were still talking, Straw looking increasingly dejected, Ripley turning on a smooth act.

'Depends on whether Dugdale's crowd want to use him or not,' Bulman said. 'He could finish up in Parkhurst, or taking over the pigeon training job for Whitehall.'

Lucy laughed and shook her head. 'I've met Scobie Beasley. She'd commit murder rather than allow that to happen.' There was a moment's pause. The murmuring of voices went on across the loft. 'So if Rosy didn't kill the Professor,' Lucy said, 'who did? Straw?'

'I don't think so . . .'

Ripley finished speaking and came over to Bulman. He dropped to a crouch before them and spoke in hushed tones. 'Right. I've got all I need out of Straw. He's being co-operative. Got no choice, really. The Manchester K.G.B. chap is coming to service a L.L.B.'

'L.L.B.?' Bulman queried.

'Live Letter Box,' Lucy said, and grinned when Bulman glanced at her in amazement.

Ripley said, 'It'll happen tomorrow. Early. At eight in the morning my office is going to mount a quiet surveillance operation. We'll record the guy on video-tape, tail him back to his camera shop, which Special Branch will in the meantime have raided.'

Bulman shook his head. There was something he didn't understand. 'Why wrap up something you've known about for so long?'

Ripley stood up and smiled. 'All good things must come to an end. Jack Straw doesn't want to play any more, and he was a critical link. The Professor's dead. We may as well charge the local Soviet agent and kick the thing into touch.'

'What'll happen to him? To Jack Straw?'

'Banged up for life.'

'And the local spy? What's his name, Selwyn?'

Ripley gave an ironic little laugh. 'He'll be tried, of course, then sent back. Doubtless exchanged for some poor tourist on a three-day trip to Leningrad.' He looked down at her. 'Thanks for all your help.'

'My pleasure,' Lucy said coldly.

Ripley added, 'No need for you to hang around. Your job's done. We can take over from now . . .'

Bulman stood up, saluted, and without a word, as angry and as cold as Lucy, climbed down to the ground.

Peter Ripley was in position, on a warehouse roof, by six in the morning. Two Special Branch men were with him, and by radio they positioned four more on the ground. In Manchester itself, the raid on Selwyn's shop began immediately the green van slid away from the kerb outside.

Two cameras were in place down below, well concealed, waiting for their first glimpse of the K.G.B. man as he drove along the deserted road.

It was bitterly cold. A heavy dawn mist hung over most of Manchester, and the docks and warehouses themselves looked bleak and dead.

The tramps were still sleeping. A single fire burned, a solitary figure huddled by it, poking at it. The newspaper-clad shapes of the others were dotted around in the lee of the higher walls.

Ripley turned his binoculars on the usual set-down point, a stack of railway sleepers by an overgrown pair of rusting metal tracks. The dog belonging to the female dosser was nosing around down there. Ripley didn't suppose that mattered too much. A pile of old boxes had been thrown down by the sleepers, and the dog was sniffing around them. It lifted its leg and pissed against the cardboard, then padded off in search of scraps.

'Here he comes,' someone whispered, and Ripley turned the glasses to the road.

Selwyn expected nothing. He drove slowly across the waste ground, then came around the old sheds and coal bunkers and bounced across the tracks. He stopped as he always stopped, but this time, perhaps because it was so chill, remained in the van. He opened a copy of the *Sun*, then fumbled in a pack of cigarettes.

He lit the cigarette that he removed, then crumpled the pack and tossed it onto the pile of sleepers.

'That's it. That's the box . . .'

'What happens now?' the S.B. man asked.

'What would normally happen is that Straw will come down, put London's message tube into the pack and give Selwyn time to run it through his decoder before sending it on. Selwyn will go away for an hour, then return. We'll wait to get the pick up . . .'

Selwyn looked around the wasteland, then folded the *Sun* and chucked his cigarette out of the window.

He started the van's ignition . . .

The boxes moved. A dishevelled, black-clad figure clambered out of them, and ran the two paces to the van, wrenching open the door. Watching from on high, Peter Ripley could only gasp his surprise.

'Who the hell's that?'

Through his glasses he managed to answer his own question. 'Bulman. George Bulman. What the hell's he playing at?'

'Making a citizen's arrest by the look of it,' one of the policemen said. 'Look there . . .'

Distantly, blue lights flashed.

'Damn Bulman!' Ripley said.

Two police cars came into view, parted company and approached the green van from two different directions.

There was something of a struggle for supremacy going on down below; Selwyn had a knife. But George Bulman was a Master of his Art: he elbowed the K.G.B. man three times in the throat, and the plump figure of the spy slumped heavily to the ground, gasping for breath.

'And then there did gather all the mighty Dogs of War . . .' Bulman intoned. He was standing with Desmond O'Dowd and Lucy, watching as a long, black Ministry car drove slowly, almost silently, into the scene of the arrest. Bulman didn't have to look too hard to see Bill Dugdale's rotund features staring at him from the back seat. The woman with him he didn't know, but guessed to be Scobie Beasley.

Selwyn was raising his voice, objecting strongly as two large-built Manchester policemen bundled him into their car. Peter Ripley and the men from the Special Branch stood looking glumly on. They had had a brief to film the spy; they had no brief to arrest him, and no brief to prevent his arrest.

'For murder,' Lucy said aloud.

'And attempted. Don't forget the attempted murder.' Bulman glanced at her. 'Damn near got me with that stiletto of his. Hidden behind the rear-view mirror.'

'He killed the Professor, anyway,' Lucy said. 'That's enough to send him down.'

Desmond O'Dowd – who, on Bulman's instruction, had called the police at precisely seven forty-five – extended his hand and Bulman shook it gladly.

'So the old boy's at least got justice. I'm glad of that, George. And I reckon we can find the extra eight quid to pay your water rates in full.'

'Magnanimous to the end,' Bulman said. 'But I can't say the same for justice, Desmond. That bird will fly like one of Straw's pigeons. Straw would have been next on his hit list, by the way.'

'How so?' Lucy asked.

'The Russians had got wind that they were being conned. The whole operation was doomed from about two weeks ago. That's why the Professor got terminated.'

'Poor Prof . . .' O'Dowd said.

'Poor Rosy,' Bulman murmured.

'Tell you something,' Lucy added. 'The Funny People don't seem very thrilled with you.'

They all looked towards the approaching shape of Dugdale.

'So what's new?' Bulman said.

But William Dugdale was beaming all over his face. 'Well, George, I see you got your man.' The woman with him simply scowled. Bulman noticed that she kept looking up, searching the sky . . .

'I trust it hasn't spoiled your little game,' Bulman said sardonically.

'On the contrary,' Dugdale said with a boyish grin. He walked with Bulman back towards where the tramps, including Green Hat, were sitting around a good, high fire. 'Murder is murder, George. We had our job, you had yours . . . you beat us to the pinch. So it goes.'

'Glad you can be so philosophical.'

'Oh by the way,' Dugdale said suddenly, 'Scobie here is very worried about Santiago . . .'

'Santiago?'

'Yes. A pigeon. It should have checked in yesterday, but she can't find it.'

'One of your pigeons is missing . . .'

'Precisely.'

Bulman chuckled. 'Oh dear, oh dear . . .'

Scowling at him, Scobie Beasley said, 'What's the joke?'

'I'm afraid your pigeon's fulfilling a rather different role, now . . .' He nodded towards the group of tramps. 'Cheerio, Green Hat!'

Green Hat twisted round, saw Bulman, and waved his hand.

'Cheerio, Quiet. Good luck.'

In his hand he held a spit. On the spit, nicely roasting, was the blackened carcase of a small bird . . .

PART THREE

A Cup for the Winner

Chapter Twelve

Nothing seemed to be going right for S.T.G. Investigations these days, and when they *did* go right they didn't pay. In the few weeks since the Jack Straw affair, Bulman and Lucy had handled only four minor cases, and they'd paid almost as badly as that last murder hunt.

What was annoying Bulman at the moment was that he'd been played for a sucker. He arrived back at the shop, early in the morning, after a long and uncomfortable night waiting for the man who had last hired him. Harry Patterson owed him three hundred and sixty pounds expenses, for doing a 'little' job that had taken Bulman to an oil rig in the North Atlantic.

But Harry Patterson was broke. He'd been broke all along. He didn't have the money to pay, but he had the criminal instinct to try and threaten Bulman.

After a cold night, to be threatened by a cheap crook had just about finished George Bulman. He'd been a little tough on the man . . .

Patterson owed him a favour, now. At that particular time of the morning that particular fact did not seem particularly important, or even welcome. It would soon turn out to be quite useful.

He picked up the mail that was strewn just inside the door, but there was nothing of interest among it: just bills. He inspected the tall Georgian mantelpiece clock that he'd been working on the day before, and to his great satisfaction the mechanism was still going strong. He touched two moving parts with a little oil, then made himself a cup of tea and sat down at his desk.

He switched on the telephone answering machine, and as expected there was the usual chaotic message from Lucy which she always left when going away for a day or two.

'George, it's me. I've left two Scotch pies from Harrods in the safe. The refrigerator's broken and that's the coolest place. So don't call the bomb squad. The do at the Magdalen Disaster Club goes on until breakfast so don't wait up. I'll do the VAT when I get back . . .'

Bulman frowned as her voice ended. 'Magdalen Disaster Club . . .?' Lucy was in Oxford, visiting her old tutor, one Don Porter, now lecturing at Oxford University, and no doubt romancing fifteen to the dozen about her favourite hobby, Mediaeval History. Part of Lucy, Bulman knew, still missed the subject. Her small living space, at the back of the shop, was crowded with the books and papers that she'd been using on her course in St Andrews, and many was the night she would be up until four, just reading.

There was a second message. An American voice, male, addressing him with all the impersonal detachment of someone who is quite used to treating people as machines.

'Mister Bulman, my name is Wilbur C. McLeod. Would you please call me at the United States Embassy, 499 9000. I have some work for you. Thank you.'

'Well, about time,' Bulman muttered, and reached for the phone to call the number. It was just after eight thirty in the morning and the cool woman who answered told him, very curtly, that no one at the Embassy accepted calls until after nine.

Bulman made more tea, then started to prepare a good, large grilled breakfast. He was beginning to feel human again, even though the Patterson tussle had left him shaky and angry.

Three hundred and sixty quid! I could just have done with that. Bloody Patterson. But I'll make you earn that debt, my friend . . .

At a minute to nine, just as his eggs were sizzling nicely and about ready to be eaten, the phone rang.

'Damn . . .'

He turned the electricity off below the pan, picked up a sausage and chewed it as he went back to his desk.

The call was from McLeod.

'I was about to call *you*, sir. What can I do for you?'

'I have a rather precious item I need tracing, Mister Bulman, and you may be the man for the job. Could we meet at Grosvenor Square at . . . say . . . ten o'clock?'

'Ten thirty would suit me better. But that's fine.'

'Ten thirty, then. Goodbye Mister Bulman.'

Definitely more like it, Bulman thought to himself, as he quickly finished breakfast, bathed, shaved, and made his way to the centre of the city.

He arrived on time, and picked McLeod out straight away. The man was sitting on a bench, hands in his coat pockets, staring idly into the middle distance. He wore gold-framed glasses, and had a thick head of dark, well-groomed hair. He stood up as Bulman approached him, watching the newcomer quizzically. Bulman thought how excessively American the man looked.

'Mister McLeod, nice to meet you.'

'Mister Bulman . . .' they shook hands and McLeod smiled. 'I knew you'd have no difficulty finding me.'

'The art of detection is to know what you're looking for.'

'Quite so.' McLeod started to stroll around the gardens of Grosvenor Square, away from the majestic building that was the Embassy. 'You know, the circles I move in, I get to hear things.'

Walking in step with the tall American, Bulman smiled and shook his head. 'And what circles would they be, sir?'

'In the course of my work. George Bulman, I've heard, is one of the last true detectives.'

Laughing, Bulman said, 'Some praise at morning what they blame at night.'

'But always think the last opinion right,' McLeod finished, and both men chuckled. 'Alexander Pope.'

'Pope, eh? I never did know who'd said that.'

'I think it was Pope . . .'

They strolled on. McLeod continued, 'Mister Bulman. I asked to meet outside the Embassy because, while I need the services of a good and honourable detective, the problem is a personal one.'

Bulman jumped to the obvious conclusion. 'Blackmail.'

'Not at all. I wish to recover a family heirloom. A very valuable item, which was stolen from us.'

This was more like it. Bulman stopped and tugged his notebook from his pocket. This was more up his street, a search in the true Holmsian tradition. Clues, interviews, travel . . . a real case!

'You don't mind if I take notes,' Bulman said, and McLeod shook his head. 'What exactly *is* the item in question?'

The American stopped and turned to face Bulman. His eyes twinkled behind his glasses, and he smiled evenly. 'It's a golden quaich. Several hundred years old.'

'A golden what?' Bulman said. He'd never heard of the thing. The word sounded like a cross between 'quake' and 'quech'. He couldn't begin to imitate the sound of the name.

'A *quaich,*' McLeod repeated, and spelled it out. 'It's a Loving Cup. Quaich is Gaelic.'

'A golden cup.'

'A *solid* gold cup. It was given to an ancestor of mine by Callum Lamont, who was one of the King's minstrels.'

'I see.' Bulman scribbled the man's name down, even though he doubted there was much point. 'And when exactly was this . . . cup, when was it stolen from you?'

McLeod said, 'Precisely ten of four in the afternoon, Wednesday the fourteenth of April.'

Bulman scribbled it all down. 'Wednesday . . . fourteenth . . .'

'Seventeen forty-six.'

He had written the figure before it occurred to him to think about what he had written. He stared at the notepad, then looked quickly up at the American. 'I hate to tell you this, but the trail may be a trifle cold by now . . .'

They sat in the lounge of the Britannia Hotel and drank coffee. McLeod told Bulman the whole story, as he had himself pieced it together. His enthusiasm was infectious, and helped dispel all Bulman's puzzlement at the incongruity of an American consul behaving like an over-eager stamp collector.

In Wilbur McLeod's own words: he was just another Yank with roots fever. Since he'd arrived in Britain he'd traced three half cousins and six fifth cousins, all with the same name, and got the beginning of a family tree going back to the 'auld hame' in Poc' and Bhui, in the Highlands.

The Loving Cup, the quaich, had been stolen by Captain Caroline Scott, a lowland Scot himself in the service of the English. A traitor, a mercenary, a man with no feeling for his people, but a great instinct for capitalizing upon the time of English oppression.

'He was, like all of his lowly kind, the scourge of the Highland Jacobite Clans. You never knew who or when to trust, and Scott took full advantage of that. He was in the service of Billy the Martial Lad, as he was known . . .'

'A villain,' Bulman guessed.

'The Duke of Cumberland. Son of King George the Second.'

'And this Scott nicked the family whatsit.'

'He butchered the whole family,' McLeod said, his voice lowering slightly. 'Fourteen men, women and children. Bayoneted mostly. The men he hung from the roof beams of their houses. Then he burned the whole village around them, and left with the treasures not just of our family, but all the clan families . . .'

'A right monkey.' Bulman scribbled notes. 'And you, Mister McLeod . . . are you the rightful heir to this quaich?'

McLeod shook his head. 'I doubt that. But I *am* a true descendant of the murdered family. Hell . . . I'm sure I am. I've researched it so damned thoroughly. I've visited the site of the affair . . .' he produced two photographs that showed moorland scenery, and in the middle of it the clear stone ruins of a small village. He looked wistful. 'I'm kind of . . . attached to Hector and Janet McLeod of Poc' an Bhui . . . I feel like I know 'em. They're friends, Mister Bulman. Friends across two hundred years. To get the quaich back would be a sort of . . . a sort of revenge. On Scott.'

Bulman nodded, understanding that such sentimentality was quite normal among Americans in their ancestral lands. 'And you want me to track it down.'

'I know it's a long shot. But I hear that you are a man for a challenge. And I'm still looking myself, and between us we might get a lucky break.'

'What if I locate it?'

'Then offer to buy it. I've become fairly well known among collectors of Jacobite memorabilia.' He waited for Bulman to grasp the significance.

'And the price would go up, you mean.'

'People do know of my little weakness,' McLeod confessed. He straightened up, reached into his coat pocket and drew out an envelope. 'This is an advance. Two thousand dollars. Take it, I'm sure you can use it. Wilbur McLeod is no carpet bagger. I like to pay my way fairly.'

'Well thank you very much, sir,' Bulman said, accepting the envelope with great enthusiasm. 'I'll do my best.'

McLeod stood, and they shook hands again. 'Please do your damndest. And let me know if you need more funds. Right now, affairs of state call. But I'll be in touch regularly.'

While Bulman had been up west, Lucy had arrived home from her Oxford do. If she was hung-over, it didn't show. She was busily hoovering the shop floor, working with gusto, her hair tied up in a scarf, her face set grim.

'Gordon Bennett,' Bulman muttered as he stepped into the offices of S.T.G. 'What's happening?'

Lucy didn't look at him. She seemed angry, and she worked the vacuum nozzle below her desk. 'I'm attempting to make my living and working conditions – combined, please note – just a little more tolerable.'

Bulman walked across to his desk and watched his slim companion as she beavered away on the cleaning. 'Well, don't spoil its character, Lucy.'

She stood up abruptly, and fixed him with a furious stare. 'George, it's all just too . . . too quaint! We're mature people, you know. But what're we surrounded by?' Her Glasgow accent became more pronounced the more angry she got. 'Stuffed ducks! Dismasted Schooners in glass cases. *Dusty* glass cases. Grotesque Victorian chamber pots! George, it *is* seedy.'

'Seedy?' he said, picking up on a word which was an unfamiliar one for Lucy. 'Who've you been talking to?'

'I haven't,' she said crossly. Then she looked a little apologetic. 'How did you know?'

'I'm supposed to be a detective. Who's been gettin' at you? Your old tutor?'

She nodded. 'He's trying to get me to go back. Back to Mediaevals. Says my sort of work must be seedy . . .'

'Well he's dead wrong.'

'Yeah.' She brightened up. 'Anyway, a spring clean won't hurt, even though it's October.' She stared at her boss. 'Did you get the money from Patterson?'

'Nope.'

'So what happens now? We lie about the VAT?'

'Pay it with these . . .' Bulman said, and tossed the envelope towards her. Lucy picked it up, tore it open, and beamed when she saw the packed dollar bills.

'Great! What've we taken on? Mafia?'

He shook his head, watching her quizzically. Scottish girl, Mediaeval scholar . . . she might have some inside knowledge that might help.

'What do you know about Captain Caroline Scott . . .?'

Lucy frowned, thinking hard. A trick question? 'She plays the . . . *tambourine*,' she guessed. 'For the local Sally Army band.'

'The one I'm thinking of was a chap. Seventeen forty-six.'

And Lucy *did* know who he was talking about. '*That* Caroline Scott.'

'You've heard of him?'

'A butcher. He interpreted George the Second's instructions to lay waste rebellious Highland clans with the gusto of a high Tory Joseph Stalin. Nasty piece of work.'

'Well,' Bulman added, 'It seems that he nicked this bloke's quake . . .'

'This bloke's what?'

'A quake. A haggis-chomper's Loving Cup.'

With a laugh, Lucy corrected his pronunciation. 'A quaich.'

'Precisely. And our client – Wilbur McLeod – wants to trace it. Beginning from seventeen forty-six.'

Lucy looked astonished. 'Not much chance of fingerprints, then.'

'Exactly what I thought. What we need's somebody with a touch on the antique gold trade.'

Lucy took off her headscarf. 'You do that bit. I'll do the history side. That bloke at Oxford, my old tutor, Don Porter . . . he's a good historian. I'll call him back and see if he can recommend some Jacobite Scholars.'

'Only if they're not too seedy.'

Lucy pouted at him. 'So I'm young and impressionable.'

'And what about the belated spring clean?'

She grinned. 'Have you forgotten how to work a vacuum cleaner, then, George Bulman?'

Bulman immediately went in search of a friend of his, an ex-colleague from the Fine Art Squad. He knew exactly where to find Evan Reid, and wasn't disappointed.

Reid was sitting in the corner of the plush lounge bar of the Bunch of Grapes, a pub in the Aldgate. He was about thirty-five years old, but was one of those men who might be anything from twenty to fifty. It was the way he presented himself, the way he dressed . . . the way he dyed his hair bright blond. His clothes were expensive and what Bulman called 'tres chic'. He wore a small gold earring in his right lobe.

Evan Reid looked nothing like the Detective Superintendent that he was.

'Wotcher Elsie,' Bulman said, as he came over to the small man. Reid looked up and effected a very 'affected' look of surprise.

'Well, well, well,' he said in his richly cockney tones. 'Wot you doing down this way, George? I always think of you in more, um . . .'

Bulman said, 'Use the word "seedy" and I might take grave offence.'

'Colourful locations,' Reid concluded, with a broad smile.

'Wot you drinking, Else? Moscow gin as usual?'

'Large one, Georgie. Ta.'

Over drinks, they nattered about old times. 'How's life in the Fine Arts Squad?'

'Just wonderful, George,' Reid enthused. 'Got me Super, didn't I.'

'I heard.'

'Only acting rank. But it's a bit more mazullah. 'Ow 'bout you, big George?'

'Can't complain, Elsie. Tell me.' He leaned forward across the table. 'Gold quakes. Lot of 'em about are there?'

'Gold what?'

'Quakes. Jock items, Loving Cups. Generally given by minstrels to chieftains . . . Kings to minstrels. That sort of gear.'

Evan Reid gave a broad look of understanding. '*Quaichs!*' he said loudly.

'That's the word,' said Bulman.

'Mostly Scottish silver. Or other metals. Gold's very rare. Don't find many of those.'

'This one belonged to Hector McLeod. It was nicked in seventeen forty-six by some plundering redcoat.'

Reid nodded, almost as if he knew the very incident that Bulman was talking about. 'Probably Caroline Scott . . .'

'Bit of form, ad 'e?'

'Nasty ponce,' Reid agreed. 'Sadistic with it. You're not getting into the fencing game, are you George? That would be embarrassing.'

Bulman was incensed by the suggestion. 'Sod off, Else. I've been retained to trace it to its present location. Starting from its last known owner. This Scott person.'

Evan Reid sipped his vodka and thought hard. Suddenly he nodded, slammed his glass down and pulled a pen out of his inside pocket. He tore the top off a beer mat and scribbled a name. 'Try this bloke. Name of Moriarty. He's got four brothers, in Hong Kong, Rome, Los Angeles and Edinburgh. He's your ace Celtic artefact and precious metal man. If the cup isn't still with the Scott family, he's your best chance.'

It had never occurred to Bulman that the quaich might still have been in the hands of Scott's descendants. A logical place to start . . .

'Evan, you're a brick.' He drained his own drink and stood up. 'Let us know if you have any further thoughts.'

'Will do. That was a good vodka . . .' Reid fiddled with his glass. Bulman grinned. To the barman he said,

'Another vodka for the gentleman. And make it a small one this time. He's driving.'

While Bulman was sipping spirits with the weirdest policeman in the Met, Lucy was calling up Don Porter at Oxford.

'I must confess,' Porter said, after a few minutes of trying to convince Lucy to come *back* to Oxford, 'Mediaeval Scotland is a closed book to me. To tell you the truth, the term Mediaeval is not something I generally apply to the country.'

'I know,' Lucy said wearily. 'We were all running around in sheep skins, stealing each other's cattle.'

'You know that's not true,' Porter said quickly. 'The Celtic culture north of the Wall had some fascinating systems and conventions.'

'I was hoping,' Lucy said, 'That you could help with some contacts.'

Porter laughed. 'And I think I can. He's a touch unusual. But a brilliant Scottish expert. His name is Professor Sabuto Matsushita.'

'Matsushita? Any relation to the Campbells?'

'I think he could be the man for you. I'll give you his address. He's in London, so you shouldn't have far to go.'

Matsushita wasn't teaching that afternoon. He was relaxing. Lucy took her shoes off and was conducted to the edge of the Kendo Hall, where the Professor was unwinding after a hard few days. As she watched, she began to wonder whether or not Don Porter was having an hysterical joke at her expense.

Two men stood motionless in the middle of the hall. They both wore black silk robes, belted at the waist, and leather body armour. Their faces were covered with the dark grills of Kendo masks. Each held a long, wooden sword, and was standing in an awkward posture, the sword towards his opponent.

They suddenly moved. They rushed at each other, screaming like banshees, and struck and weaved and dodged and struck again, seven or eight immense blows . . .

And as quickly as it had begun, it ended. Each man straightened up, bowed, and turned away.

The Japanese Professor walked over to Lucy, removing his mask. He was a balding, cheerful looking man, his grin more teeth than lip. He bowed quickly to her, and made to walk by, but she said, 'Are you Sabuto Matsushita?'

'Matsush'ta,' he corrected courteously. 'In Japanese we do not pronounce the letter I.' Again he bowed, but he looked at her quizzically. 'You wish to learn the art of Kendo?'

'Not really. I'm not sure, actually, that I've got the right Professor Matsush'ta . . .'

'Matsush'ta not a common name in these parts. Very rare. I'm sure I'm only one . . .'

'I'm actually looking for a Scottish history expert . . . is that you?'

The small man chuckled. His eyes twinkled. In a deadpan voice he misquoted: 'Poor wee cowrin', timorous beastie. What a panic-O's in thy breastie. Would the Lord the gifty gie us, Tae see oorsel's as ithers see us . . .'

And as he finished the quote, he emitted a loud, and very Japanese, *'Hei!'*

Chapter Thirteen

Unlikely though it would have seemed to the casual onlooker, Matsush'ta was a veritable mine of information on the Jacobite period of Scottish history. He took Lucy to a curry house, and indulged in a vindaloo, one of the hottest meals on offer. He talked non-stop. His interest in Scotland had begun in his youth when he had seen the Japanese film *Throne of Blood*. On learning that it had been based on Shakespeare's *Macbeth*, his fixation with the northernmost Celtic lands had begun in earnest.

He knew all about Captain Caroline Scott, and he had a very fair idea of how to contact the various surviving branches of the family, although he warned that it was unlikely that they would be quite as violent as their infamous ancestor; so no cold revenge . . .

Lucy, gratefully, returned to the shop late in the evening. George Bulman was there, humming softly to himself as he played jazz through his Sony Walkman.

Evan Reid's contact, Moriarty, had been useful too. He was a man who kept assiduous records, mostly in old Jacobs cream cracker tins, but he had been an expert on the Celtic gold trade – a trade which functioned at a desperately low level; there was bronze and silver, but very little of the yellow stuff – and had helped Bulman enormously.

He had given the Private Investigator a list of auctions, antique dealers and fine arts dealers who would be most likely to handle such gear as a Loving Cup.

'Lists and lists,' Lucy said hopelessly. 'We'll be a year chasing all of these down, me and the Scotts, you and the dealers . . .'

But Moriarty had also produced the photocopy of an

original sale notice, dated April 2nd 1887. It was advertising the sale, by Stevens and Sons of Cumberland Road, Derby, of one gold Scottish Loving Cup.

'Eighteen eighty-seven!' Lucy said with mock excitement. 'We're hot on the trail now.'

Bulman had to admit that the task looked increasingly daunting. McLeod had put up two thousand dollars as an advance, and that was certainly worth a bit of leg-work, and phone chasing. But by talking to the various experts in the field, Bulman had come to realize just how *vast* the antiques world was, how easily the description of the Loving Cup could be wrongly made, and how thoroughly like seeking the proverbial needle seeking the 'quaich' was becoming.

He had reckoned, however, without McLeod himself. McLeod had been searching for this cup for years; he had gone to S.T.G. Investigations, he had told Bulman, out of a sense of frustration, and the need for a break from his obsession. He had come close, he had said, and lost the trail . . .

But as Bulman and Lucy assessed the task before them, and found it overwhelming, McLeod called the office, and the lucky break was in . . .

After speaking on the phone to the American, Bulman came through to the small back room where Lucy was making their late night chocolate.

'Sounds as if the bugger's doing our job for us,' he said, but he was not unhappy.

'McLeod?'

'The very same. He's had a report of the Loving Cup changing hands in nineteen sixty-seven. In Cheshire, to one Lady Valentine Eggar. She bought it for two thousand seven hundred pounds, from an antique dealer now deceased. No other details. I can get the old dear's address from Burke's . . .'

'Nineteen sixty-seven,' Lucy muttered as she stirred the chocolate drinks. 'Hell's teeth, George, we hadn't even got into the twentieth century.'

'I'm not complaining.'

'It's not right,' she said. 'The client beating us to the draw.'

'Remember, he's been at it for years. This is a lifetime interest. Ta . . .' He accepted his drink, then frowned as he saw the expression on Lucy's face. 'What's up?'

'Have you checked this bloke McLeod out?' she asked meaningfully.

'Absolutely,' Bulman replied. 'He's registered on the Diplomatic List. Senior bloke, Legal Section. In fact, he's a senior counsellor in their legal department.'

'You've used a few Job contacts . . .' Lucy said, and Bulman grinned.

'Better safe than sorry. He has excellent degrees. He was a partner in the Washington law firm of Boone, McLeod and Hoover. Independently wealthy. Married to Mamie Van der Het, whose family own half of Manhattan.'

'And his interests?' Lucy sat on the table and sipped her chocolate. Bulman had been a thorough wee mannie . . .

'He's a Scottish freak, no question. He turned up at a Windsor Castle reception in full Highland dress, the McLeod tartan proper to the stitch.'

With a smile, and swinging her legs down to the floor again, Lucy said, 'Well. You've put my mind at rest. What happens now? After a few welcome hours sleep, I mean?'

'I'm off to Cheshire,' Bulman grinned. 'To meet a Lady.'

Lady Eggar was as charming a hostess as any that it had been George Bulman's privilege to encounter. A tall, slender woman, in her mid forties and highly attractive, she invited Bulman to stay to lunch, and Bulman accepted without thought.

Nonnington Hall was an impressive, if slightly rundown stately home, and in all the time that he wandered through its corridors and gardens with Lady Eggar, he hardly saw a soul. Two gardeners and a single groom, taking care of the several horses in the stables.

The stables were, if anything, better kept than the house itself.

But Lady Eggar turned out to be a false lead. It was not her who had inherited the Loving Cup – among other valuable items – but her Great Aunt. When that particular lady had died, Lady Eggar had inherited the title 'sideways', and with it the most appalling debts.

The cup, along with many other objects that had been with the family for between ten and two hundred years, had been sold to allay both death duties, and maintenance bills.

Bulman returned to London and met Wilbur McLeod late in the afternoon, a pre-arranged meeting that McLeod himself had set up.

McLeod was disappointed, that much was clear to Bulman, but he took his disappointment philosophically. They strolled around Grosvenor Square gardens in the early evening, and it was McLeod, if anyone, who was trying to bolster *Bulman*'s spirits.

'All these false leads are part of the game,' he said. 'I've been searching for years, I don't expect everything to fall into place in one fell swoop. Keep your chin up, Bulman. I feel we're encroaching upon the quaich with every hour.'

Bulman smiled. 'If it was sold in nineteen sixty-seven there'll be a record of the direction of the sale. My partner's with the Eggar family solicitors in Lincolns Inn Fields right now.'

McLeod nodded thoughtfully. 'That's good. I really am most impressed with the *verve* with which the two of you have gotten down to this case.'

They turned back towards the Embassy. Lights were coming on, and dusk was descending in chill folds of grey. 'Do you believe in hunches, Bulman?'

'Indeed I do, sir,' Bulman said.

'Well, I have a hunch you're going to find this damn

"quaich". I'm beginning to get the feeling I always get when something breaks for the best . . .'

Bulman smiled, thinking of the way his knee tended to tingle when things were about to break for the worst. 'It certainly looks more promising,' he said. 'Thanks to your own good work. I feel as if S.T.G.'s rather been dragging along on your coat-tails.'

McLeod chuckled. 'Team effort, Bulman. That's what I always tell them at the Embassy. Team effort I always say, and here it is, working again . . .'

'Has anyone ever told you that you sound like Ronald Reagan?'

McLeod didn't detect the sardonic nature of the statement. 'Why, he himself told me just that. The President himself. Wilbur, he said, I sure as hell love the sound of your voice. How come, Mister President, I asked. Because you sound just like me, son, he said.'

McLeod laughed at his own joke, and Bulman smiled dutifully. He was getting cold. It was time for home, for some clocks, for a large gold watch . . .

'Have you had many dealings with us Yanks, Bulman?'

'Off and on.'

'Mostly cops, I expect.'

'Mostly villains,' Bulman corrected. 'In my old job you tend to meet the seamy side.'

'Indeed,' McLeod agreed. 'And since then?'

What was all this about, Bulman wondered, but he went along with the idle chat. They were close to the Embassy, now, and McLeod had a meeting in five minutes. 'Just yourself, really,' he said. 'And one right cheeky ponce.'

'A cheeky ponce?' McLeod said, emphasizing the cockney sound of the expression. 'What's that?'

'A con-man. Name of Elias Greenstein. He took a U.S. bank for a couple of million. I nearly had him twice.'

'Bad luck.'

'Got to respect him in a way,' Bulman said softly. He

hadn't thought of Greenstein for some weeks. Perhaps he'd been blocking the memory of the last fiasco out of his mind. 'He enjoys the game,' he went on. 'A bit like us . . .'

'Moriarty and Sherlock Holmes.'

'Bit like that, yeah.'

They stopped at the Embassy steps and shook hands. 'Well I have to brief the Ambassador, now. Duty calls and it's going to be a long night for me . . .'

'I'll call you if anything comes up.'

'I'll call *you*,' McLeod insisted. 'I'm a difficult man to get hold of sometimes . . .'

'I *had* noticed that,' Bulman said. 'And your secretary never seems to pass on messages.'

McLeod rolled his eyes, a silent gesture of despair. 'All the more reason to meet outside the hallowed ground . . . So long, Bulman.'

'Cheers . . .'

The offices of the solicitors who represented the Eggar Estates were like something out of a Dickens fable. Cramped rooms, old desks, piles of musty papers, and walls lined with leather-bound books which gave off their own distinctive odour. Lucy sat on the other side of a battered mahogany table from Samuel Lane, a middle-aged character who himself might have stepped from the pages of Nicholas Nickleby. He was turning the heavy sheets of a vast ledger, and running his finger down the lines of handwriting that appeared thereon.

At last he nodded and smiled. 'Here it is. Ostrich egg, mounted by Faberge . . . what on earth would that be, I wonder . . . an Old Saxon salver and bronze dish . . . and a gold something. It looks like "quich".'

'Quaich. Loving cup. That's it exactly . . .'

Lane read the small amount of information recorded with the entry. 'Scottish in origin, reputed to be the property of the Scotts of Linlithgow. Acquired during the rebellion of seventeen forty-six.' He peered over his half-frames at Lucy. 'Does that sound like the particular item that interests you?'

'Acquired!' she was blustering. 'Captain Caroline Scott butchered an entire village to cover his tracks.'

Lane stared at her, then pursed his lips, trying to sense the significance of what she was saying. 'Possibly. Possibly. They say there was a lot of that sort of thing about in those days.'

Lucy decided not to argue with that indifferent sentiment; she decided not to mention her great hero, the French Knight Boucicaut, who, though a Crusader, never butchered an innocent family in his entire life. She simply said, 'Does the ledger record to whom the quaich was sold?'

'Yes indeed . . .' Lane crossed to the other side of the vast tome. 'Here we are. Disposed of by the Eggar Trust to the Caledonian Society of Bloomsville Pennsylvania. June the tenth. Nineteen seventy-six.'

'Oh no . . .' Lucy said, seeing their goal slip away from them.

'However. An export licence was denied. It was sold again, for the sum of four thousand, eight hundred pounds, to the Jacobite Society of Magdalen College, Oxford.'

Where she had been just a few nights ago!

Lucy stood up quickly, beaming broadly. 'Mister Lane, God and his angels guard your sacred throne. And may ye be thrice blessed!'

Lane looked pleased. 'Why, thank you. Glad to have been of service. I'm afraid there'll be a small search fee . . .'

In the heart of the U.S. Embassy, behind the half-glassed door with his name and his rank upon it, Wilbur McLeod worked late on two aspects of the Italian Trade Delegation's application that had been overlooked during the meeting that afternoon. It was work he loved. That he would be late home could not be helped.

McLeod was a stocky, balding man, who peered at the world through thin, silver-framed glasses. His face was pale, the result of pill-taking to keep his blood pressure down, but he had about him the look of a man who had over-indulged his tastes in an earlier, safer time of life.

He looked up as his secretary, Bonnie Kowalski, knocked and entered his office. She was an attractive young woman, from the same home State as he, and they had a good working relationship. She placed a plate of biscuits on the desk by his right hand, and two typed letters for his signature by his left.

He looked at the biscuits, then up at her and smiled. 'You knew I was working late . . .'

'I had a sort of feeling,' she said, and grinned. 'But I'm off home.'

'You do that. Goodnight, Bonnie.'

She turned to go. He looked up again and said, 'By the way. Any more calls from that guy . . . what's his name?'

'Bulman,' she said. 'No sir. Just the two so far. But he *is* making a nuisance of himself. I'll get security onto it if you want.'

McLeod lounged back in his chair and shook his head. 'Not worth it. Just keep him at arm's length. I get nervous when strangers ring me up.'

'Don't worry,' Bonnie said. 'You're permanently in meetings as far as that guy's concerned.'

'Good girl,' McLeod said. And then the second thing occurred to him. 'Damn . . . can you wait a minute? I wanted you to post a letter for me.'

She came back over to the desk, smiling. 'Sure.'

'It's that letter from Hector McLeod of the McLeod Society.' He fumbled among his papers, then found his cheque book. He quickly scanned the content of the letter, a polite request from the Clan Chairman to a man who may well have been descended from the same Clan, for a donation of about twenty pounds for the restoration of the McLeod Chapel, on the Isle of Skye.

'I can't refuse *these* guys a simple request like that,' he said, and smiled. He scribbled the cheque – for fifty pounds sterling – and signed it with a flourish. 'If you wouldn't mind, Bonnie?'

She accepted the cheque and the letter, and smiled. 'Not at all.' Glancing at the letter she frowned. 'The address is a hotel in Bloomsbury . . . is that right?'

McLeod shrugged, looking back at his work. 'Hell, Bonnie, I can't see someone trying to rip me off for that sort of money. It's probably just their London base. Send it and don't worry about it. I sure as hell ain't.'

The net was tightening around the McLeod family's Loving Cup. The trail, once so cold, was now getting almost hot enough to excite George Bulman. Things were fitting into place rather nicely . . .

Too nicely. It was a thought that had been nagging at him for some hours, a thought that had reached his knee – which was tingling on and off and causing him discomfort. The case was fitting together with just a little too much ease. There was no challenge.

And as Bulman arrived at the premises of the Jacobite Society, in Oxford, something Lucy had said to him a few hours before – 'Maybe the challenge will come later' – was still a sentiment that he couldn't shake off.

It had that ring of prophetic genius about it. When she had spoken the words, his knee had twitched.

When things seemed this easy, look for a catch . . .

But for the moment he was being entranced by the small, delicately built, and delightfully chirpy young woman, Miss Fiona Lamont, who was junior curator of the Society's museum. She led Bulman through the small premises towards the room marked 'records'. But Bulman slowed and inspected the unfussily displayed artefacts and objects, and found them fascinating.

The museum was a single room, with glass cases in its centre, in which were brooches, medals, cups, coins and small weapons. Around the walls, in larger display cases, was an impressive array of Scottish banners, broadswords, scraps of tartan and flintlock rifles. The place was pristine, not a speck of dust out of place. It was not stuffy, either. It was like being in someone's sitting room, full of interesting conversation pieces.

'You've maintained this place beautifully, Miss Lamont,' Bulman complimented her, and she looked pleased.

'Museums can often be boring simply because they try to show too much, without enough information.'

'I quite agree.'

She said, 'We're kept going by a grant from the Carnegie Trust, and the Royal Historical Society. But that money only just covers our running costs.'

Bulman picked up a huge broadsword from one of the wall displays. He grunted with the effort of raising its blade to the horizontal, and Fiona smiled. The blade gleamed, well polished and protected against rust.

'Are you any relation to Callum Lamont,' Bulman asked as he carefully placed the sword back on its rack. 'The minstrel?'

Fiona looked astonished. 'Fancy you knowing about Callum Lamont! Yes,' she went on. 'I think I am. Very distantly, of course.'

Bulman said, 'There was a quaich . . .'

'A Loving Cup. Yes . . .'

'Given by Lamont to one of the McLeod Chieftains. Some time ago.'

With a smile, the girl said, 'Twelve seventeen A.D.'

'Good Lord.'

They strolled on towards the records room. Fiona said, 'All the Lamonts were harpists. They brought the *Clarsach*, the small, Irish harp, to the halls of the

Scottish Chieftains. They became very popular, very welcomed, and very rich.'

'And Lamont, C., gave the Loving Cup as a sort of return gift . . .'

Fiona shrugged. She unlocked the door of the records room and led Bulman into the airy but tiny office, its walls covered with box files. 'Who can tell? But the story is that it was made of gold, so it was an important gift all right.'

'And now it's here,' Bulman whispered, impressed by the span of time, by the history embodied in that simple vessel.

Fiona Lamont said, deflatingly, 'I'm afraid not. It was sold, I know that . . . to help with financing. All this was before my time, but I know for a fact that several items were acquired from an estate in Cheshire—'

'The Eggar Trust . . .'

'And sold almost immediately. There hadn't been the funds available.'

'Damn. So it's gone again.' A horrible thought occurred to him, as he watched Fiona flipping through the bound sheets of a box file marked 'Sales'. Perhaps, after all, it *had* gone to the Caledonian Society of Pennsylvania . . .

His fears were unfounded. McLeod's treasure edged a foot or two closer. Fiona said, 'Here we are. The Lamont Quaich, presented by Callum Lamont, minstrel to King Robert the Bruce, to Roderick McLeod of Poc an' Bhui, in thirteen seventeen . . .' she looked up, guiltily. 'Sorry, I was a hundred years out.'

Bulman chuckled. 'We'll let you off. This time.'

She read on from the sales notice. 'Looted by Captain Caroline Scott on April fourteenth . . .'

'Seventy forty-six.'

'Precisely. It was then acquired by the Jacobite Society in August nineteen seventy-six – from the Eggar Trust, as I thought – and sold *only last year* . . .' again she looked up, apologetically. 'Sorry again. I thought it was sold before my time.'

'Never mind. Who bought it?'

'Walter Lewin and Sons. Antiques and Heraldic Items; they're at fifteen Queen's Row.' She closed the file. 'Well there you are. Walter Lewin and Sons supply the auction rooms. They buy objects, do them up, get them talked about, and then sell them through Sotheby's, or more likely a small auction room called Stevens & Sons.'

'You're an angel, Miss Lamont. You have aided my quest enormously. Can I, er . . . treat you to a spot of lunch?'

She smiled with delight at the idea. 'I always find detectives fascinating. Will you mind if I ask you some personal questions?'

Bulman looked at her and rued the age difference. *Youth, remind me of thy sting . . .*

'Not at all . . . Fiona . . . it will be a pleasure.'

While Fiona Lamont fetched her coat, Bulman used her phone quickly. Lucy's words of the evening before – maybe the challenge is to come – and the pat way that he had picked up the tracks of the Loving Cup, both of these things combined to make him almost positive about one thing and one thing only: that the gold quaich would be going up for auction within the next few days! Something which, though it would seem to be coincidence, would be anything but.

He got through to Evan Reid at the Fine Arts section of the Met. 'Elsie? I need a favour. It's George . . . yeah, I'll buy you a *very* large vodka, tonight, when I get back. Right. Listen . . . there's a bloke at the U.S. Embassy, name of Wilbur C. McLeod. A legal counsellor. Be a good chum and ferret out his home address, will you? It's very important.'

Reid agreed.

Fiona Lamont stood waiting for him by the door. He walked with her into the streets of Oxford, with a spring in his step.

*

In any scheme that was worth its metaphorical salt, there was always one big risk, and one big chance. The risk in Elias Greenstein's latest little game was still to come; but the chance, the little gamble he'd taken, was about to pay off.

He heard the sound of the postman working his way down the street, and peered through the window of his small hotel room. It was a seedy hotel, in a part of Bloomsbury that did not fit well with the up-market image of that particular part of London. Most of the clientele, here, were live-in types, mostly girls, and a few single men of dubious reputation.

Greenstein had had a room here for years, under the name Angus Wells.

He had expected the letter from Wilbur McLeod – the *real* Wilbur McLeod – to have arrived yesterday, and had felt mildly disappointed when it hadn't. And yet, Greenstein felt that he knew his man well enough. How *could* a McLeod, and especially one who was so fascinated in his family history, refuse so simple a request for cash? Greenstein had researched the man thoroughly. So thoroughly that he had become quite fascinated in the history of the quaich himself! It added a certain pleasure to the game, an extra and unexpected interest; it also made him confident that his act, with George Bulman, was as authentic as it could be.

Greenstein chuckled at the thought of the Private Investigator, telling *him* all about the 'cheeky ponce' he was after. Telling the cheeky ponce *himself*, and not even realizing that he was walking inches from the man he'd been hunting for months.

The mail dropped through the box downstairs, and Greenstein left his room and trotted down to fetch it. One of the wretched girls from the basement rooms was already there, sorting through it. She was wrapped in a towel, her hair still wet from showering. Greenstein regarded her with disgust.

'Nothin' for you, Mister Wells,' she said, with a cold look at the man who always ignored her. Without her make-up on, he thought, she looked like a figure made out of white putty.

She was holding the letters, challenging him to disagree with her. He held out his hand, and after a sullen moment she passed the small bundle to him. He turned from her, sorted through it quickly, and to his secret delight found the letter from the U.S. Embassy . . .

He took it out of the pile, threw the rest of the mail onto the side table, and went upstairs.

'Who's letter are you pinchin'?' the disagreeable girl asked, her voice a mocking statement of her contempt for him.

'Mind your own goddamn business,' Greenstein said in his most forceful Brooklyn accent.

Back in his room he quickly opened the letter, and drew out the cheque. 'Fifty quid. You generous old sucker!'

Laughing, he went to the bedside table and unfurled a small roll-pack of instruments and vials of fluid.

He selected a very thin-bladed scalpel. He held the cheque to the light, and scrutinized the writing and the spread of the ink. As he thought, McLeod had used a fine-writer. The ink hadn't spread, and probably hadn't gone deep.

He colour-matched the background paper of the cheque with a combination of the various water-colours that were in the pack. It took him nearly an hour to be satisfied that the shade was precise.

Then he dipped the scalpel into the solution and began to laboriously scrape at the words 'Hector McLeod Chapel Trust' and 'Fifty pounds only'. He used a tiny series of special sponges to soak up the loosened ink.

When he had finished, he had a blank cheque.

It took very real effort to see the ghostly outline of the original writing.

Chapter Fourteen

At this precise moment in time two things were oppressing Lucy McGinty. One was – as usual – George Bulman's infuriating tendency not to tell her everything that he knew, or suspected, or was doing. Something she had said the day before had set him thinking hard; some internal 'break' had excited him; *something* had happened, but try as she might she could not get him to let her in on the secret.

'You've got a brain, girl. Work it out for yourself.'

He was *the* most *infuriating* man!

The other bane of Lucy's life at that time was her old tutor, Don Porter. Ever since she had attended the reunion of the Mediaeval Society, up at Magdalen College, Porter had been nagging at her to return to her studies, to get back among the academics.

She was both pleased and irritated by the man's insistence. It was very flattering. It was also very inclined to make her insecure. She had taken the decision to quit her studies, and pursue the life of a Private Investigator, with the sort of spontaneity that many people call 'haste'. She had dropped four years' courses, all her friends, and a great future as a lecturer and researcher in Mediaeval British History, for a career which Don Porter had concisely summarized as 'seedy'.

The doubt as to whether or not she had done the right thing had never, really, gone away. What had seemed like a glamorous change in direction was nothing of the sort. It *wasn't* seedy; far from it. But it wasn't anything like what she'd expected.

She had thought of herself as the assistant to the last of the great detectives: deduction, research, confrontation, reward. The reality of her job was legwork, persistently repeated questions, lucky breaks, and a great dependency upon the police.

Don Porter, now a Don at Oxford, had immense respect for Lucy's academic abilities, and her natural flair for the subject she had been studying. It was not his fault that he genuinely believed she had made a mistake in quitting.

He was not to be blamed for his sudden persistence in trying to entice her back, to work with him at Oxford itself!

It was, nevertheless, damned irritating – and very confusing – to find him waiting for her, at the Clock Shop in Shanghai Road . . .

She parked her car, pulled out the two bags of shopping from the back seat, locked up and walked quickly towards him, fumbling for the keys to the shop. Bulman was in Oxford. She had been chasing up several of the branches of the Scott family, but without success.

'Hello Don,' she said wearily. 'What a surprise.'

'I was afraid I'd miss you,' he said. He was in his early forties, a striking looking man, his long hair quite grey, his features sharp.

'Have you got more information on the Celtic gold cup?'

'I'm afraid not,' he said, as he followed Lucy into the shop. He looked around. 'So this is it.'

'Bulman Clock Hospital and S.T.G. Investigations combined. In all its seedy glory.'

Porter wandered about the office as Lucy unpacked her bags, watching her ex-tutor with a mixture of apprehension and irritation. He picked up Bulman's latest piece of reading. 'The Psychology of Thirteenth Century Chivalry', he read aloud. 'I'm glad you're keeping your hand in . . .'

'It's not mine.'

Porter put the book down and followed her through to the back room. 'Lucy, the reason I came round –'

'To do a spot of slumming?'

Porter shook his head at her determined irritation. 'Listen, you droll Scottish person. I need to encourage talent. It's part of my job.'

He reached into his coat and produced a large, double-paged form.

'I've already done my VAT return,' she said drily.

'This is an application form to be examined for matriculation, in the Department of Mediaeval Studies at Magdalen College, Oxford.'

She hesitated, looking first at the form, then at him. He was offering her the sort of opportunity that most scholars would regard as an impossible dream.

Be firm, she said to herself. Be resolute. 'I'm happy doing this.'

'Hell's teeth, Lucy. You're wasting yourself. Most Mediaeval scholars . . .'

'I'm no longer a Mediaeval scholar,' she snapped. The phone began to ring.

Porter said, 'Give it another chance, Lucy. Listen, next Friday evening the Mediaeval Society's running a lecture.'

She looked at him, half amused, her eyes twinkling. 'Next Friday?'

'On Boucicaut.'

'Boucicaut.'

'Your favourite Crusader. Why don't you come?'

With a grin, Lucy said, 'Get thee behind me Satan.' Then she moved quickly to answer the phone. Porter heard her say 'Mister McLeod? Oh hello. George Bulman has been trying to get you at the Embassy . . .'

Porter walked back into the shop, peering at the clocks and other objects that cluttered the shelves. He was feeling despair. It had been a wasted journey. He was about to take a discreet and quick leave, as Lucy talked, when a stocky, short-haired man, with outrageously long side-burns, stepped in through the front door.

Bulman, of course.

'Being looked after?' he asked, and Porter explained

who he was. He was still holding the book on Chivalry, and Bulman noticed this and frowned. 'Good book that . . .' he said.

Porter looked down and nodded. 'Mediaeval History. I suppose Ellery Queen's more in your line.'

'Why?' Bulman asked, instantly cold.

'Crime fiction.'

'Never touch it. Hello Lucy.'

Lucy was off the phone. 'Where have you *been*, George Bulman?'

'Out and about. This case is getting curiouser and curiouser. Who was that on the dog?'

'McLeod.'

Bulman chuckled. 'Was it, indeed? What did he want?'

'He says he'd like to meet you at the Embassy. Ask for him at the Marine Guards desk. He'll send someone down for you.'

'Terrific,' Bulman said pointedly. 'I've got some very good news for Mister Wilbur C. McLeod. This is one meeting I wouldn't miss for the world.'

Lucy took a deep breath, and expressed her annoyance by exhaling it noisily. 'Well are you going to tell me, or not?' she said, hands on her hips.

'All in good time, Lucinda. All in good time.'

He turned away, nodded a curt goodbye to Porter, and went outside to hail a taxi.

Far from gaining access to the hallowed ground of this little piece of America, as Bulman trotted up the side steps towards the Marine desk he saw McLeod watching him from inside the foyer. McLeod smiled, waved and came through the doors to meet him, shrugging into his long black overcoat. He was carrying a briefcase.

'Let's keep it outside the Embassy, shall we?' McLeod said. 'Walls have ears etcetera. I'll take you to a good pub.'

Once ensconced in the corner of the Grosvenor

Arms, warmed by good Scotch, Bulman told the American the good news.

'You've found it?' McLeod said with soft delight. 'You've really found it?'

'Strangely enough, it wasn't all that difficult,' Bulman said drily.

'But this is marvellous! Let's get round to those antique dealers right away. I smell success!'

'Not quite there yet, sir,' Bulman had to tell him. 'The cup is being auctioned.'

McLeod looked worried, polishing his gold-framed glasses anxiously. 'Auctioned, eh . . .'

'Tomorrow. By Stevens and Sons of Mayfair.'

'Tomorrow?'

'Word is it'll go for anything up to fifteen grand. In sterling.'

McLeod looked very slightly crestfallen. 'I never doubted it. And if they know I'm in the bidding it might go even higher . . .'

Bulman sipped his drink, waiting for a moment as McLeod gathered his wits. He said, then, 'So do you want me to go and bid for it for you?'

McLeod slapped a hand on his knee, a sudden resolve. 'You bet your sweet ass I do!' Bulman looked slightly shocked by the description, but McLeod had suddenly found a new lease of enthusiasm. 'Listen, Bulman. Here's what I'm gonna do. I'll give you a certified cheque. Right? I'd give you cash but the bank's in the City and I'm up to my butt in Spanish Trade legislation.'

He opened his small attache case, and Bulman heard him tear a cheque from a cheque book. He closed the case and placed the cheque on the top, fumbling in his pocket for a pen. Bulman noticed that the cheque was already signed.

'This is how it goes,' McLeod said. 'I'll write this out for fifteen thousand pounds. I'll make it payable to cash. You take it to your bank first thing tomorrow. Clear it with the First National Bank of Alabama in the

City. I'll telephone and make all the necessary arrangements. Then we meet at Stevens and Sons, but you do the bidding. I'm known to be a Scottish nut and we don't want to get milked, right?'

Bulman considered it all. He inspected the cheque, then nodded in agreement and pocketed it. 'All sounds very sensible, sir. But what if the bidding goes over fifteen grand?'

'Then I'm out,' McLeod said emphatically. 'Wilbur C. McLeod knows when he's beat. I'll take the money from you and go sulk.'

'You trust me with this?' Bulman asked, his voice hushed.

'All the way,' McLeod said. He reached out his hand. Bulman shook it, then rose from the table and went back to the shop.

At nine thirty the following morning, Bulman was up, shaved, bathed and dressed, and ready for some very special action. He could hear Lucy's voice downstairs. She was on the phone to the London branch of First National Bank of Alabama. Bulman waited for her to come upstairs. He sang merrily to a record of Purcell's 'Dido and Aeneas' and regarded himself in the mirror as he fixed a rosebud in his lapel.

He was wearing a plum velvet jacket, a cream poplin shirt, a silk scarf and dark trousers. He placed a broad-rimmed felt hat on his head and adjusted the angle, inspecting his appearance most critically.

Lucy came upstairs, yawning. She stepped into his room and her eyes nearly popped from their sockets with astonishment.

'In the name of the wee man!'

'What's the matter with you, Lucinda?' Bulman asked in a tone that implied how dare she imply criticism of his disguise.

'George, isn't that a bit over the top?'

'The essence of detection is to blend in, Lucretia,' he said in an authoritative voice. 'Those auctions are frequented by the rich, by the sophisticated, by the—'

'Eccentric?'

He scowled at her. 'Believe me. I'll look the bleedin' part. What's new? Not that I need to ask.'

'McLeod has a credit balance of one hundred and sixty-three thousand pounds. Plus much the same in his dollar account. His bank parted with the information surprisingly easily.'

'I don't doubt it,' Bulman said, inspecting himself again in the mirror.

'All in all Wilbur McLeod checks out as a model citizen, and his reputation at the Embassy is very high.'

'Very high indeed. Wilbur McLeod is one of the straightest, one of the most upright, one of the staunchest . . . I didn't doubt it for a minute.'

'George,' Lucy said wearily. 'You're being damnably mysterious. What *is* going on? That bank shouldn't have spoken to me on the phone so easily . . .'

'I told you before. You've got a good brain. Work it out and you'll win a coconut.'

He picked up a green plastic bag, buttoned up his velvet jacket, and led the way downstairs. Lucy followed, muttering, 'Riddles, riddles, riddles. And what's in the plastic bag?' The bag contained something bulky, she could see that. 'Isn't that a bit incongruous?'

'Something for later,' Bulman said. 'And it's perfectly congruous.'

They went straight to Bulman's commercial bank, and went into the Manager's office. The auction was at eleven o'clock and they didn't have much time.

'Are you sure a plastic bag is the safest place for fifteen thousand pounds, Mister Bulman?' the Manager asked anxiously, as he accompanied them to the street. The wad of notes was bulky, and the plastic carrier bag looked perilously insecure.

'Perfectly safe. Don't worry. Thank you for clearing the cheque so fast . . .'

'Not at all. Mister McLeod had confirmed his instructions at opening time this morning. I must say, these Americans certainly know how to cut corners.'

Bulman chuckled. 'Yes indeed, sir. They certainly do.'

Bulman and Lucy made the auction rooms with minutes to spare. Stevens & Sons were a small, posh firm, and their auction room itself was more like a hotel suite than a salesroom. About twenty people sat in plush chairs around the raised platform, where a young man with bright eyes and a nervous mannerism conducted the auctioning in a brisk, almost matter-of-fact way.

McLeod was standing discreetly at the back of the room, trying to keep himself unseen. That he was there at all seemed, to Lucy, to be monstrously stupid, if he *was* worried that his interest would push the price of the Loving Cup above its commercial value.

The thing that she noticed most, however, and it was a fact she would have found hugely amusing if it hadn't been so embarrassing, was that every one else in the auction room was dressed in sober, dark grey suits, even the two women who sat there.

Bulman stood out like a purple bruise on a corpse.

She hardly had time to mutter a livid 'I told you so', however, since the Quaich came up for sale, and the action started.

'Item twenty-six on the catalogue. A beautiful Scottish Loving Cup, made in thirteen hundred and eight by Gregor Gow of Inverness. More renowned for his work in Scottish silver, but this Loving Cup, for many years held by the Eggar Trust, can truly be said to be a stunning example of his work . . .

'It was a gift to Callum Lamont, the harpist, from King Robert the Bruce. And subsequently handed down, through a *sept* of the McLeod clan. What am I bid, ladies and gentlemen? Shall we start at six thousand pounds?'

Perhaps because of its beauty, and its full history, there was a rapid spate of bidding in hundred pound jumps from about six of the buyers. Bulman stayed out. Lucy noticed that a rather attractive young woman on the same row of seats as them was bidding quite frantically, and looking increasingly irritated as the price reached ten thousand pounds. Her face had reddened and she was biting her lip in earnest.

Curious, she thought. Very curious.

At twelve thousand pounds everyone but this particular young woman had dropped out. Lucy saw her smile, then look anguished as the price jumped to twelve thousand five hundred. George Bulman had caught the auctioneer's eye, and discreetly rubbed his left ear. The woman tried to look around to see who was bidding against her, but she couldn't do it *and* remain discreet.

The auctioneer was asking for the second time. She raised a finger.

Twelve thousand seven hundred and fifty.

Bulman scratched for another two fifty. Thirteen thousand.

The girl shook her head, then slumped in her chair, looking terribly crestfallen.

And the quaich, Callum Lamont's gift to a Clan Chief, came to George Bulman . . . wrapped in newspaper.

There were other items for sale, of course, but Bulman and Lucy rose and quietly stepped into the front shop area. The young woman who had tried to get the cup for herself had already left.

McLeod was waiting there. Clutching his green plastic bag, with the paper-wrapped cup inside it, Bulman crossed to him. 'Mister McLeod. Excellent day's work!'

McLeod looked very nervous, glancing around and indicating that Bulman should keep his voice down.

Bulman bellowed on. 'No need for secrecy now, sir. Surely.'

'I like to remain anonymous,' McLeod said. He looked at the carrier bag. 'Is that it?'

'That's it. Here you are, sir . . .' Bulman delved into the bag, brought out the cup and raised it high. It glinted in the shop-room lights. A beautiful and elegant piece of goldwork. Wrapping it again, Bulman passed the green carrier bag to the American, who accepted it quickly and with a brief smile.

'A moment, sir,' Bulman added, as McLeod shook hands and made to bustle away. The American frowned, turning round nervously. 'Don't forget your change, sir . . .'

'Oh. Of course . . .'

He came back towards Bulman, who held two thousands pounds in twenty pound notes. In his other hand he held a sheet of paper. 'And of course . . . our bill.'

'Oh. Right. How much?'

'Two thousand pounds, sir.'

'Two *thousand* . . .' For a moment McLeod's face darkened, then he took control again. 'That's a lot of money.'

'A lot of travel. Search fees, solicitor's fees, daily fee, two people, engaged full time. It's all here, sir. All itemized.'

McLeod smiled and relaxed slightly. He said, 'Well. I guess so. You've earned every penny.' He took the bill, folded it and slipped it into his pocket, then hurried away towards the entrance to Stevens & Sons.

That he was rattled certainly helped what happened next. As he opened the door, a man barged past him, knocking him off balance.

Lucy said, 'That's that rat Patterson. The man who owes us!'

'He's paying us,' Bulman whispered grimly.

Patterson was carrying an identical green carrier bag to McLeod, and both bags had fallen when the two men had collided. Bulman watched, impressed with the smoothness of the operation, as Patterson quickly picked up his *own* carrier bag and gave it to the shaken American. McLeod shook off Patterson's attempts to dust him down, and apologize. He scurried away. Patterson, looking cold and unhappy, came over to Bulman.

Bulman drew a large, white Marks & Spencer's carrier bag from his jacket pocket, opened it, and Patterson dropped the green bag, and the Loving Cup, into it.

Without meeting Bulman's eyes he said, 'All square, then?'

'All square, you rat,' Bulman whispered. 'And don't tell me that wasn't the easiest three hundred quid's worth you ever earned.'

Patterson sneered. 'Drop dead, Bulman.'

'Back to the gutter, ratbag.'

Patterson left, his debt to S.T.G. paid off. Lucy shook her head, staring at her boss. 'George Bulman . . . how low can you stoop . . .'

'Come on,' Bulman said. 'We've got to see a man about a quaich.'

They were expected at the U.S. Embassy, and conducted upstairs by a tall, stiff-backed Marine. When they reached the door marked 'Wilbur McLeod', the Marine left them, and a young woman conducted them through to the Counsellor's office.

It was the same young woman who had been bidding so hard at the auction. She stared at Bulman with deep suspicion, and before Bulman and Lucy were taken into McLeod's office they heard her say, 'It's *them*. From the auction. It's Bulman . . .'

'That's all right, Bonnie. Send 'em in.'

Bulman entered the room, Lucy behind him. The jolly-faced man rose to his feet, a shorter, dumpier, balder McLeod than the McLeod who had been at the auction.

'How very pleasant to meet you again, sir,' Bulman said, and McLeod echoed the sentiment.

'Again . . . ?' Lucy whispered.

McLeod said, 'Bonnie, I'm not to be disturbed. Not even by the Ambassador.'

'Very well, sir.'

She closed the door behind her. Bulman took out the gold quaich and unwrapped it, passing it to the American, who almost hesitated to take it. But he took it and cradled it lovingly in his hands, and then raised it to his lips and kissed the cold metal.

'I feel,' he said, 'that the McLeod Clan have avenged a terrible misdeed. At last. My thanks, Mister Bulman. My thanks indeed for getting this.'

'It was no trouble,' Bulman said, and Lucy gasped.

McLeod said, 'So what'd the other guy get?'

With a chuckle, Bulman told him. 'An old brass bowl that's probably been around my junk shop for years. Roughly the same size and weight. By now he's probably beaten his brains out with it . . .'

Both men laughed. Lucy stared from one to the other of them, and everything fell into place. 'The other McLeod was an imposter, a con-man . . . cashing in on your obsession with the Clan McLeod . . .'

'Not just *any* con-man,' Bulman said to her, and she spoke the name in unison with him:

'Elias T. Greenstein!'

'You finally got there,' Bulman said teasingly. McLeod was still fondling the chalice. 'I admire your style, Mister Bulman. I think we should find something to fill this lovely Loving Cup with, and I have just the thing . . .' He rustled about inside one of his desk drawers and came up with a full bottle of Gleneagle Malt Whisky. He filled the cup, and raised the toast.

'Slainthe!'

'Slainthe maith,' Bulman rejoined, and accepted the cup, and drank.

Lucy watched him. '*When?*' she said suddenly.

Wincing from the superb, but lethal, bite of the Malt, Bulman said, 'When what?'

'When did you know?'

Bulman chuckled. 'I could never get through to Mister McLeod here at the Embassy, and that struck me as odd . . .'

'Thought you were a damned nuisance, actually,' McLeod said with a warm smile.

'But our inquiries gave a good report, of course, because there *was* a Wilbur C. McLeod. Plus the whole investigation was made too easy by Greenstein himself, under his McLeod alias. He *knew* where the cup was. He just wanted to con me into buying it with the *real* McLeod's money. He used all the enthusiasm, and Clan links, of Mister McLeod here, and almost pulled off a neat and satisfying scam.'

Lucy took all this in, and it all seemed so clear, now, so obvious. And that irritated her to the bottom of her Scottish heart. She said, 'But why was your secretary in the auction, bidding against us?'

McLeod shrugged. 'I'm a practical kinda guy, Miss McGinty. I wanted this damn quaich more than anything. Okay. Maybe your partner here was on the level, maybe not – begging your pardon, Mister Bulman – but the important thing was that I got the cup. If you'd skipped with the money, then Bonnie there was instructed to bid up to twelve five. That would have got it all right, I was sure of that.'

Bulman watched Lucy, amusement on his face, twelve-year-old whisky warming his insides. 'I smelled a rat the moment I didn't even get my messages passed through to this office. So I chased up Mister McLeod's home address, saw that he wasn't the monkey who'd hired me, and together we worked out this little scheme.'

'That's why the bank was so co-operative,' Lucy said. 'You *yourself* told them to co-operate.'

'Greenstein called in twenty minutes later. Even if Mr McLeod here hadn't called the bank he'd probably have got away with it,' Bulman said. 'He's a clever bastard.'

'Why did he do it?' Lucy asked. 'Why such a small game? He must still be living off of his American Bank con. It makes no sense . . .'

'It does to Greenstein,' Bulman said quietly. He took the quaich from McLeod again, sipped it and raised it, as if to an absent friend. 'You said it yourself, Lucinda. For the game. The game of winner and loser. The thrill of it all. This time he lost. Next time . . . who knows . . . but there's going to be a next time, and we'll get him with something a little more . . .' He glanced at McLeod, who suggested,

'Gaolable?'

'The very word. When Greenstein goes away, I want him to go away until Kingdom Comes . . .'

Lucy took the cup from him, swigged at it and spluttered.

'Right, George Bulman. Let's go home. You and I are going to have a little chat!'

Chapter Fifteen

On Friday, Don Porter turned up at the Shanghai Road shop again, dressed for what he hoped would be an evening at the Mediaeval Society with Lucy, and perhaps his last chance to affect her opinion: to sway her back to Academia.

He hadn't really checked the programme, but he knew that the main talk was about her great hero, the Chivalrous Knight Boucicaut. That alone made him think that she'd at least *reluctantly* come . . .

To his astonishment, she was dressed and waiting for him, and took his arm as they sought out a taxi in the rainy evening.

They arrived slightly late, although the main event hadn't started; Porter grabbed two glasses of claret, and Lucy a handful of sausages and cheese on sticks. They moved through into the lecture theatre, which was quite full.

Lady Eggar was on the stage, talking to someone. As Porter and Lucy took their seats, proceedings began to come to order.

Porter couldn't understand why Lucy kept chuckling, why there was such a mischievous gleam in her eye.

'Who's the old lady?' Lucy whispered.

'That's Lady Eggar. She's President of the Mediaeval Society. Does all the touting for speakers. Lucy, this is where you should be. Among your peers!'

Lucy sipped her claret and grinned. 'I must say, it's great to be hearing about Boucicaut. He's my absolute hero!'

'I just want to show you what you've been missing, working in that seedy shop with that . . .'

'With that what?' she challenged him.

'That very odd relic of Victorian Detection . . .'

'Ssh.'

The chatter in the hall had subsided. Lady Eggar cleared her throat and introduced the evening's topic. Lucy settled back expectantly, and Porter crossed his legs, preparing for what he secretly imagined would be a very tedious evening.

Lady Eggar said, 'My Lord, Ladies and Gentlemen. The fourteenth century Crusader, Boucicaut, is the subject of a most learned paper, based on the psychology of the Crusade Ethic, and we are indeed fortunate to have here, to read his own work, shortly for submission to the Open University . . . Mister George Bulman!'

The hall echoed to a burst of applause. Bulman, who had been sitting in the front row, stood up and rather nervously walked onto the stage. He gripped the lectern with gloved hands and blinked out at the audience over his half-framed glasses.

Next to Lucy, who was shuddering with suppressed laughter, Don Porter's mouth was open, his face an hilarious mask of utter astonishment.

'Exceptio probat regulam . . .' Bulman began, 'de rebus non exceptis.' He paused and looked around, then smiled. 'I think we can all agree with that, don't you?'

Lucy almost spluttered her amusement. There was a ripple of laughter in the hall at Bulman's little joke . . . all except from the dumbfounded Porter.

'The ethic of chivalry was nowhere more alive,' George Bulman was saying, 'than at the court of Charlemagne . . .'

It was a long and splendid evening.

George Bulman, speaking to the Society at Lady Eggar's request, was absolutely in his element.